Careless Whispers

Careless Whispers

ROCHELLE ALERS

A STARLIGHT ROMANCE
Doubleday
NEW YORK   LONDON   TORONTO   SYDNEY   AUCKLAND

A Starlight Romance
Published by Doubleday, a division of
Bantam Doubleday Dell Publishing Group, Inc.
666 Fifth Avenue, New York, New York 10103

A Starlight Romance, Doubleday, and the portrayal of the letter S are
trademarks of Doubleday, a division of Bantam Doubleday Dell
Publishing Group, Inc.

Library of Congress Cataloging-in-Publication Data

Alers, Rochelle.
Careless whispers.

"A Starlight romance."
I. Title.
PS3551.L3477C37   1988   813'.54   88-14973
ISBN 0-385-24496-7

*To Benjamin and Noemi—for their prayers and patience,
and to*

*the Ladies of Summer on Marlborough Road—for their
support and spirit.*

Thoughtless words can wound as deeply as any sword, but wisely spoken words can heal.

Proverbs 12:18 *Good News Bible*
—*Today's English Version*

Careless Whispers

ONE

Dyana felt the ripple of excitement as soon as she pushed open the glass doors to enter the reception area at Westgate Publishing. The general mood was pulsing with an almost circus-like excitement. She likened the electricity surging through the magazine's offices to opening day at the World Series, Super Bowl Sunday or the anticipation of watching every lingering, anxious-filled second as the apple inched its way down the pole to light up a new year at Times Square.

The crush and warmth of human flesh was overwhelming, given the less than adequate space to accommodate the crowd which had gathered. Cigars, cigarettes and pencils hung loosely between fingers of one hand while the other gestured wildly or gripped Styrofoam cups filled with the distinctive aroma of coffee. Rising spirals of blue-gray smoke lingered in the air, clouding the recessed lighting in the corked ceiling. Journalists and photographers leaned against the wheat-colored textured walls, lounged in love seats and chairs and some had affected squatting or sitting positions on the carpeted floor.

ID badges, hanging from lapels, collars and pockets indicated most major New York newspapers and periodicals were represented. Dyana silently acknowledged a correspondent from *Newsweek* with a smile as she began to push her way through the crowd. Most were speaking quietly to the person nearest them, but the sound escalated steadily until it resembled a monotonous drone.

She avoided a protruding elbow and tapped a broad back covered by a lightweight beige jacket. "Excuse me."

"His unorthodox tactics are deliberate and dramatic," the

man explained to a shorter, slender man hanging on to his every word.

"You're crazy if you think *Souls of the Children* was a piece of Hollywood."

"I'm not referring to that piece. It was his first, so he hadn't developed his flair for theatrics."

"What about the photos? They were haunting and definitely conscious-provoking," the short man argued. "They were powerful enough to turn even Westmoreland and Haig into pacifists. I can't understand why you don't like Bradshaw."

Thick shoulder muscles bunched up under the beige jacket. "He's an opportunist!"

Dyana had heard the epithets "opportunist," "power-seeking," "brilliant" and "dictatorial" bantered about the offices of *Pinnacle Magazine* and Westgate Publishing for the past two weeks.

The magazine was bracing for its new editor in chief, and the publishing world was holding its breath. The publisher of both the magazine and book company had successfully negotiated the luring of Nicholas Bradshaw away from *The New Yorker,* with the expectation that his name and Pulitzer award-winning credentials would give the slumping magazine the sales boost it needed to exist beyond the next fiscal year.

The odor of coffee, sweet pastries, cigarettes and differing colognes clinging to bodies and cheeks bombarded her nostrils, threatening to make her sick.

"Hey, Dyana!"

Dark hair, highlighted with golden brown and red highlights, brushed the collar of an ivory-white silk blouse when she spun around to see who was calling her name. Three inches of black patent heels would not allow her to see over the shoulders and heads of the taller men blocking her way.

"Excuse me, my man," the resonant voice ordered.

Within seconds an opening appeared, and she spied a set of incredibly white teeth in a dark familiar face. "Douglas Jenkins," she sighed, reaching out for the large hands of the football-player-turned-reporter for the city's leading black weekly, the *Amsterdam News*.

"Faint on me, Dee," the low voice commanded.

Dyana looked up at Douglas as if he had suddenly lost his mind. Her mouth parted slightly. "What?"

"Faint, woman!" he rasped in her ear.

His arms curved around her waist and even if she hadn't felt faint, she did when he tightened his grip. She sagged against a muscular chest and within seconds was swept up into his arms.

"Let me through!" Douglas shouted.

All conversation in the corridor came to an abrupt halt. A pair of shapely legs encased in sheer black silk nylons and narrow pumps hung over the arm of the tall black man shouldering his way through the crowd.

The man in the beige jacket stared, blue eyes caressing the length of legs and the flowing fabric of black silk crepe de chine sweeping around Douglas Jenkins's thigh. "Lucky stiff," he mumbled under his breath. He watched the flutter of thick lashes against unblemished mahogany-colored cheeks, feeling put out that it wasn't him playing the macho role of holding a beautiful woman in his arms. It would've made his assignment a lot more exciting than being packed like a sardine in a corridor to wait for a press conference with Nicholas Bradshaw.

"You're safe, Dee."

She opened her eyes, smiling up at the grinning face above hers. "Now that was very naughty, Doug Jenkins."

Douglas raised his eyebrows. "It worked, didn't it?"

A delicate manicured hand patted his chest. "Yes, it did. You can put me down now."

Douglas's dark eyes softened and narrowed. "I'd rather hold you, Dyana. It takes me back . . ."

"Now, Douglas," she ordered softly.

He hesitated, but recognized the glint of seriousness in a pair of large golden brown eyes. "Yes, *Ms.* Randolph." Bending slightly, he set her on her feet.

Dyana smoothed out the pleats in the sweeping circle of

black falling midway down her calf. Long lashes shielded
her eyes when she adjusted the front of the matching jacket.
Her lashes swept up when she tilted her head to stare with a
brooding look at the tall man.

"Thank you, Doug. I mean that."

Douglas sighed, his mouth tightening under the trim line
of a moustache. "It's always thank you." A frown furrowed
his forehead. "You have enough brothers, Dee. You don't
need another."

Dyana turned, staring at the streams of sunlight pouring
into the window in the small office. What Douglas Jenkins
failed to realize was that she had always thought of him as a
brother. He and her older brother had attended the same
college, and many times during the four years they'd shared
a dorm room, Doug had come to Philadelphia to stay with
the Randolphs. His feelings for her had always been more
than brotherly, but what he didn't realize was that those
feelings were not reciprocated.

"It's not going to work, Doug. It didn't work ten years ago
and it's not going to work now," she tried explaining.

The muscles bunched up in Douglas's firm jaw. "Are you
still dating Michael Dalton?"

She spun around, the circle of black billowing out around
her legs. "What's that remark supposed to mean?"

Douglas's eyes went hard, cold. "Nothing, Dee," he mumbled. "Forget I said it," he snapped, turning on his heel and
walking out of the office. The solid slam of the door echoed
his departure and anger.

Her hands curled into tight fists; compressed lips and
closed eyes mirrored her frustration. Would the nasty, ugly
gossip ever stop? Would the snickering and whispers ever
cease when she walked into a room on Michael Dalton's
arm? "No," she whispered in the empty silence. It never
would until they dissolved their friendship.

She and Michael had discussed their relationship many
times over the past six years and decided what they offered
each other overrode the censuring attitudes of the narrow-
minded who refused to believe a man in his sixties could

maintain a platonic friendship with a woman in her late twenties.

Douglas's reaction wasn't much different from the others she'd encountered, only he was more polite because of the ties to her brother. She inhaled, easing the tension in her chest and softening the line along her jaw. A slight smile curved her full mouth, and her eyes crinkled in amusement. She wasn't about to let Douglas Jenkins and his cryptic remark spoil her day. She, like everyone else, wanted to see and hear the infamous Nicholas Bradshaw's plan to bring *Pinnacle Magazine* into line as a competitive literary organ.

She removed her jacket and slipped it onto a hanger. Her fingers went to the full black satin bow under the collar of her blouse, then picked at the soft pleats along the sleeve. The gossips would be given another opportunity to whisper behind their hands because she was going to play hostess at the small gathering at Michael's apartment to welcome Nicholas Bradshaw to the *Pinnacle* family.

Moving over, she sat down at her desk, focusing on a snapshot of employees of *Pinnacle* on a company picnic. This summer there would be new faces and changes. Changes—that's what the new editor in chief indicated; for her and for the magazine. It had been more than six years since she'd undergone a change. Then, at age twenty-two, she'd left an unfaithful fiancé and Philadelphia.

She arrived at her aunt's door with a single piece of luggage filled with treasured souvenirs from her childhood and a heart filled with broken dreams. Aunt Susie cradled her to her ample bosom, asking no questions and telling her she could stay for as long as she wanted. Six years later, she still lived with Aunt Susie.

Never-married Susan Randolph fussed over her when she was sick like a Mother Superior, and waved a finger under Dyana's nose when she told her she didn't want to settle down and get married.

Who's going to want you when you're old, fat and gray, child? Don't be like your aunt, baby. Loneliness is a curse.

I'm never going to get fat, and I'll dye my hair when I discover the first gray hair, Auntie.

Are you sassing me, girl?

No, ma'am. I'd never sass you, Auntie.

Both of them would laugh and Aunt Susie would take off for her beauty parlor appointment to have her hair dyed, and she would raid the refrigerator for the remains of the sweet-potato pie from Sunday's dinner. No, she would never move out and leave her aunt.

She continued to smile. She'd always hoped that Michael would find her aunt attractive enough to ask her out. The last time she'd invited him over, she noticed his eyes lingering a bit too long on Susie's generous figure.

The piercing sound of the intercom made her jump. She reached over and picked up the receiver. "Miss Randolph."

"I see you managed to wade through the sea of the curious."

"Only with help," she admitted.

"Please come down to my office. I'd like for you to meet Nick before the others get to him."

"I'm on my way."

She slipped her arms into the waist-length jacket and made her way down a corridor, away from the crowd standing outside the conference room. Michael wanted her to meet the man who was going to replace him and whom she would be working closely with in another month. She ran a hand over the smooth curls brushed off her face and knocked on the door.

"Who is it?" came a hoarse whisper.

"It's me, Dyana."

The door opened slightly and a hand pulled her through. A knowing grin on Michael's face went unnoticed when she stared at the tall figure rising from a chair. She'd seen Nicholas Bradshaw once, but he'd been too far away for her to observe him closely. The furnishings in the editor's opulent office paled by the man's presence which extinguished everything around him.

High Indian cheekbones under tawny skin, tinged with

pigments of alizarin brown to golden topaz, gave his face the strange good looks rarely seen on most men. Short curling black hair hugged his well-shaped head like a soft cap. Her gaze inched slowly down to his nose where a bump on the bridge indicated a break at some time in his life, and a strong jaw flowing into an equally strong chin with an attractive cleft. But it was his mouth, full and firm without having the appearance of being feminine that held her rapt attention.

Michael cleared his throat, breaking the spell. "Nick, this is Dyana Randolph."

Nicholas lowered his chin, tilting his head at an angle. Startling jade-green eyes swept over dark shoulder-length hair, shot through with shimmering brown and red strands. Large, clear brown eyes in a flawless reddish brown face were calm and mysterious. The raspberry gloss accented and accentuated a full, sensual lower lip. His mouth curved into an intimate smile when she raised her chin to match his steady gaze which reflected curiosity when they lingered on her slender frame. Nicholas Bradshaw had known of her involvement with the older editor before meeting her.

Dyana extended a hand. "My pleasure, Mr. Bradshaw. Welcome to *Pinnacle Magazine.*"

Nicholas grasped her smaller hand, smiling broadly to reveal white, even teeth. "The pleasure is mine, Miss Randolph."

She withdrew her hand, suddenly bereft of the warmth and strength from those long, strong fingers. So this is the Nicholas Bradshaw who worked hard and played even harder, she thought. What the press release hadn't revealed, Michael did. At thirty-seven, Nicholas had earned a string of awards and prizes for his journalistic efforts. His first book, *Souls of the Children,* a novel about the children of the Vietnam War, won him his first Pulitzer for general nonfiction. As a graduate of the Columbia University Graduate School of Journalism, he captured the Berger Award, and subsequent honors were gained for feature photography for a series of black and white prints of the people from the Appalachian region. His childhood was as spectacular as his adult life: he was born in Kyoto, Japan, when his mother joined her military-career husband in the Orient. For the next sixteen years, he lived on military bases throughout Asia, Europe and Africa, learning as many as four languages fluently. He married an actress, but the union didn't survive the year he'd spent as a photojournalist for *Life*, photographing the battles in the tiny country known as South Vietnam.

"Dyana?"

She looked at Michael for the first time, giving him her bright smile. He wasn't a tall man, but there was something about him which made him seem taller than his five feet seven inches. The sparse sprinkling of white crinkly hair covering a perfectly oval head always made her laugh when she remembered working up enough nerve to tell him his head reminded her of fluffs of meringue on a chocolate Easter egg. He'd stared at her in shock, then dissolved in a spasm of laughter, signaling the beginning of their misunderstood liaison. With Michael she always communicated her doubts, fears and hopes. He'd encouraged her to return to school to take the writing courses needed to advance in the publishing field and became personally involved whenever she needed assistance in understanding or completing an assignment. A degree in music had not prepared her for a career as a magazine editor.

"Everything is set for this afternoon's celebration," she replied, recognizing the flicker of anxiety in his eyes.

Michael dropped an arm over her shoulders, shaking his head. "I don't know how she does it, but this woman has developed a knack for reading my mind," he explained to Nicholas, who continued to stare down at Dyana.

"You sound like a talented lady, Miss Randolph," Nicholas mused as he leaned against a corner of the large desk, his hands thrust into the pockets of a pair of light gray suit trousers, pulling the fabric taut over muscular thighs.

"Multitalented is more like it," Michael insisted. His right arm slid down her arm and curved around her waist. "There's been a change in plans, Dyana." His fingers tightened on her slim body. "It's not about this afternoon's cocktail party but that Westgate has decided to hold the press conference in their offices because we'll never be able to accommodate the overflow of press."

"When are we ever going to stop being Westgate's stepchild?" she retorted angrily.

Michael released her, sinking down to an armchair and staring at a handknotted Oriental area rug. "I've explained to Nick that the book company is Westgate's favorite son, leaving *Pinnacle* to fend for itself." His head came up slowly and he looked at Nicholas, then Dyana. "I've tried to resurrect, restructure and revamp this magazine using everything I've been taught and learned in my career as a journalist, but somehow it didn't work with *Pinnacle*. Perhaps I should've let go years before."

There was a long, oppressive silence. Dyana wanted to go to Michael, hold him and tell him he was blameless. The Westgate family had poured millions into their book company to hire additional personnel and offer sizable advances to best-selling authors while failing to concede similar allowances to the magazine. The year-end profit-and-loss figures triggered a crisis when members of the publishing family were faced with the possible sale of the magazine or trying to keep it viable. Nicholas Bradshaw had become their last hope.

"You're not to blame, Michael," she said.

"I know I'm not, but the captain is responsible for his men and his ship. It's all yours, Nick. And knowing you as I do, you'll win the battle."

Nicholas continued to lounge against the desk, one Italian-loafered foot crossed over the other. Thick black eyebrows inched up when he smiled at Michael. "The battle won't mean much if you can't win the war."

A grin softened Michael's unlined brown face. "You have something, don't you?" he whispered.

Nicholas's full upper lip thinned and flattened against the ridge of his upper teeth when he returned the grin. "I'm waiting for a . . ."

A sharp rap on the door brought the conversation to an abrupt end. Paul Scranton's graying head was thrust through the partially opened door. "The equipment is in place and everyone is waiting for you, Bradshaw." Dark blue eyes danced with nervous excitement. "Good morning, Dyana," Paul offered when he noticed her.

"Good morning," she mumbled. She waited until the men filed out of the editor's office, then crossed the room to stare down at the street twenty-eight stories below.

There was nothing for her to do but wait. As an editorial assistant she was forced to defer to editors, advertising, circulation, accounting and production managers. They were the ones selected to attend the Westgate gatherings and she'd become a participant only when the occasion required Michael to bring a date; and she'd always been his date.

The brilliant June sun heated her face through the expansive floor-to-ceiling window, offsetting the cooling air flowing through air-conditioning ducts. The day's air quality was superior, allowing for a clear view of downtown Manhattan and the towering spires outlining the boundaries of the bustling financial center. She'd grown to love New York City and its people. She'd affected its fast pace, the love-hate relationship with rival baseball, hockey and basketball teams and the eclectic style that was uniquely the Big Apple.

Most people become adults when they are eighteen, but for her it had taken an additional four years. She'd lost her head and heart to her music professor and surrendered her future to him. Her father's warning that she acted capriciously when she accepted Steven Chapman's marriage proposal after dating him for only five months rang true when she was left standing in a church filled with family members and friends waiting for him to make her his wife.

After two days of crying, which had left her eyes swollen shut, and another two weeks of her brothers treating her as if she were a delicate, exotic orchid, she sat down at the dinner table and told her family she was moving to New York to live with her father's sister, Susan Randolph. It was then Edna Randolph's turn to cry when she realized she was losing her only daughter. Tensions ran high in the Randolph household, everyone blaming Steven Chapman for upsetting their harmonious existence.

Child, you can't hate the entire male species because of one snake masquerading as a man.

I don't hate men, Aunt Susie, I just don't trust them.

You must learn to trust, baby. You've got to trust someone.

Trust someone; she trusted Michael. Only Michael.

Dyana held a fluted glass of bubbly dry champagne, along with employees of *Pinnacle,* Westgate Publishing and selectively invited members of the press, waiting for Michael to make an announcement. The doors separating the living room from the dining room were opened to provide ample space for the fifty-plus people filling the spacious riverview apartment. Men had shed jackets and ties and women their businesslike suit jackets for the informal gathering.

Michael stood with his back to the glass doors leading to the terrace, the golden sun highlighting his fluffy white hair and slight physique. His voice, with a lingering trace of an Alabama drawl, was soft but carried easily in the room.

"Ladies, gentlemen, friends and invited guests." His soulful gaze swept over the assembled. "Today is a day all of us have looked forward to for a long time. Personally it means I can look forward to sleeping until noon, not having to worry about deadlines, meetings and a dwindling circulation." He waited for the laughter to subside. "But it also means not being with people whom I've come to think of as family for the past twelve years, and it means leaving people whom I've grown to love."

Dyana felt a silent shifting of eyes and her cheeks grew warm. Her expression was impassive as she concentrated on the furnishings in a totally masculine room. Tables and lamps, which were as familiar as items in her own bedroom, held her attention. She raised her chin and encountered the electric dark green of Nicholas's eyes and was drawn into the pull of the emerald orbs as they touched her face. Her pulse quickened. His gaze increased the heat in her face and she was mesmerized by the almost physical energy and fire of his eyes.

Did he also believe she was having an affair with Michael? His mouth quirked and he gave her a secret smile. He nodded, the gesture barely noticeable. He'd communicated that he understood. If he hadn't believed, he somehow sensed what she was feeling.

"Hurry, Michael. My champagne is getting warm," urged Aaron Pickering, the magazine's controller.

Michael smothered a smile. "And I can also look forward to saying things I've been forced to swallow in the past for the sake of professional etiquette. You're truly tasteless, Aaron," he declared, deadpan.

"And you're full of it, Michael," Aaron shot back. "You've been telling me that for years."

"Aaron's right," Michael continued after recapturing everyone's attention. "I've never been one to bite my tongue, and I won't bite it when I say that Nicholas Bradshaw is the best thing to happen to this magazine since its first issue nearly fifty years ago. All of you know what there is to know about the man professionally and what you don't you'll learn soon enough. I won't ask him for a long speech because he had enough of that during this morning's press conference. But I would like to welcome him to our magazine family and wish him all the best." He extended his glass to Nicholas. "Congratulations, Nick."

With a dark blue tie hanging loosely from his collar and the cuffs of a sky-blue shirt rolled back over thick wrists, Nicholas looked powerful, inexplicably virile and relaxed. His long fingers curled around the stem of his wine glass when he raised it. "To new beginnings; for all of us."

"Amen," sighed a copy editor next to Dyana.

"I'll drink to that," shouted Aaron.

Dyana took a sip from her drink before placing the glass on a table. She wasn't overly fond of the expensive wine; her metabolism always seemed at odds with the effervescent liquid. The rush was on at the tables filled with food, and she stood by waiting for an opening.

"Something wrong with the champagne, Dyana?"

The soft voice with its clipped way of enunciating sent shivers up and down her spine. It was the first time he'd said her name and she wondered why it sounded like a caress.

"It gives me a headache," she said, turning to face a solemn Nicholas.

"Can I get the bartender to serve you something else?"

She glanced at the long line of people waiting for food and drinks on the other side of the living room. "Dry white wine, please."

She found an empty chair and claimed it. She'd come to the apartment early that afternoon to prepare for the cocktail party. The florists had delivered vases filled with flowers, the wine shop cases of liquors and champagne and the caterers had set out salads, chilled shrimp, lobster and crabmeat platters and put up hot plates filled with Buffalo wings, fried rice, broiled chicken livers wrapped in bacon, barbecued ribs, rice pilaf and miniature spinach pies.

Her eyes followed Nicholas, when as guest of honor he moved to the front to fill a plate with food and request wine for her from a smiling bartender. All of his movements were smooth, no motion wasted, and instinctively she knew Nicholas Bradshaw was a man who was secure in everything he did or said. She wondered if it was going to be as easy to work with him as it had been with Michael.

"Only you'll be able to work with Nicholas Bradshaw and not swoon all over him, Dyana."

She should've known Michael wanted the *Amsterdam News* to do a piece on Nicholas Bradshaw and had invited Douglas Jenkins to the gathering at his apartment. "How's that?" she asked when Douglas hunkered down beside her chair.

Douglas fingered a curl touching her cheek, pushing it behind her ear. "Chapman really did a number on you, didn't he?" He caught her fingers tightly. "He took your love and trampled on it, leaving you empty and cautious. I know you, Dee Randolph," he rasped low enough for only her to hear. "I've watched you since you were sixteen, seeing you blossom into an incredibly beautiful woman with a lot of passion and warmth to give a man who, if he had enough brains, would appreciate it. I know you'll never see me other than an older brother, but take a bit of brotherly advice—stop wasting your youth on a man who's old enough to be your grandfather."

"Jenkins." Nicholas had returned silently. "Good seeing you again."

Douglas rose to his feet, smiling. "Same here. Do you think I can get a few words from you?"

"I can allow you ten minutes."

Nicholas's head was even with Douglas's six-foot-two frame, but Douglas outweighed him by nearly forty pounds. His large hand came down on Nicholas's shoulder. "Thanks, man. Let me know when you're ready."

Nicholas looked around the room at the smiling, animated faces of the people from the magazine, who were eating, drinking and talking in small groups. He stole a glance at his watch. "I'll meet you in the bedroom in forty-five minutes."

"You've got it." Douglas stared down at Dyana's delicate profile. "When you talk to Tom again, send my regards, Dee."

Nicholas sat beside her and she felt vulnerable, naked. Her *affair* with Michael had become like the morning's headlines, bold and screaming with their impact when everyone's attention was riveted on the tabloid's front page.

Nicholas extended the glass of wine, frowning when he noted the confident manner he'd observed earlier that morning in Michael's office slip away as she drew her lower lip between her teeth. "Did Jenkins say something to upset you?"

Her hand was steady when she took the glass from his as the corners of her mouth inched up, disarming him immediately. Dyana Randolph was back in control. Her eyes, a clear brown with a hint of gold, crinkled as she gave him an open smile. "Doug is too much like my brothers; he feels it's his inherent right to offer brotherly advice."

Nicholas balanced the plate on his knees, drawing a linen

napkin from the pocket of his shirt. He spread the square of white over her lap, then transferred the plate to her knees. She froze when his breath brushed her ear.

"Do you think of him as a brother, Dyana?"

There, he'd said it again. Why did he pronounce her name as if it were spelled Dee-ana instead of Di-anna? "No. I mean yes." She corrected herself quickly. "Doug and my brother roomed together at North Carolina A & T and . . ."

"And he has his nose out of joint because you won't give him a play," Nicholas finished perceptively.

"Why would you say that?" she questioned, staring at the length of thick lashes ringing his eyes.

"It's written all over the poor man's face. Only a blind man wouldn't see that."

She took a sip of the chilled wine. "And you feel sorry for him?"

"No." His voice was deceptively calm. "Jenkins is a big boy and if he can't get you to see things his way, it's his problem."

She picked at a boiled shrimp on the plate, using her fingers instead of the fork to dip it in the cocktail sauce in a tiny paper cup. "Doug was the first man I'd ever dated. He took me to my senior prom." She looked up, seeing his eyes widen in surprise. "My first date and my first kiss. For a high school senior, dating a college man meant I was mature and worldly."

"Which you weren't?"

"Which I wasn't," she repeated. "Once I began my own college career Doug was forgotten."

Nicholas retrieved a slice of spinach pie from the plate and took a bite. He chewed it thoughtfully, seemingly unaware that they were sharing a plate. "Apparently Jenkins hasn't forgotten you," he remarked.

"Ten years is long enough for anyone to forget."

A frown settled between his eyes when he heard her waspish tone. His strangely colored, glowing eyes traced the shape of her cheekbones, a small chin and the full lower lip, which denoted Dyana Randolph was a passionate woman beneath the elegant clothes and demure manner. "For some several lifetimes isn't enough to forget," he said very quietly.

She froze, the shrimp poised in midair. "I was speaking of people, not elephants," she quipped.

He took the shrimp from her fingertips and popped it into his mouth. "What about you, Dyana? Your obsession with not letting go of your past has allowed you to use Michael Dalton to keep men like Jenkins at a distance."

She fumed inwardly, wanting to dump the contents of her plate on his head. Apparently he'd overheard Douglas's remark. "Mind your own business," she warned. "And stop eating my food," she ordered when he reached for a piece of chicken.

He dodged her hand when she slapped at the nimble fingers snaring a spicy Buffalo wing. "You asked for wine, not food." He gave her a slow, crooked smile. "But to show you my good side, I've decided to give you my plate," he said softly.

Her mouth was still gaping when he walked away, unaware that Nicholas Bradshaw had revealed a part of himself not many saw. Just for a moment he'd lowered his guard to relax. She smiled, a dreamy expression sweeping her features. What had happened to his formidable image? Would it be as easy to work with him as it had been with Michael?

"Don't argue with me, Dyana. Why should you take a cab when Nick will drive you home?"

"I don't want him taking me home," she hissed at Michael between clenched teeth.

Michael pulled her down to the leather sofa with him. "Why are you being unreasonable?"

"I'm not being unreasonable."

"Then you're being childish."

She pulled her hands out of his tight grip. "Thanks for the compliment."

Michael folded her gently against his chest. "I'm sorry, Dyana. You didn't deserve that."

Her arms curved around his neck as she nuzzled his ear with her nose. "And I'm sorry for fighting with you. I'll let him take me home," she conceded.

He kissed her cheek, patting the soft curls on her head. "Thanks for your help, darling. As usual, the party was a success."

She nodded in agreement. "I guess it's business as usual Monday morning."

Michael pulled at the white crinkling hair over his ear. "Four more Mondays and it'll be over for me."

Dyana refused to think about not working with him. He'd been such an integral part of her tenure at *Pinnacle* that she wasn't able to imagine walking into the magazine offices and not seeing Michael or hearing his voice.

"What do you intend to do with all of your free time?"

"Golf."

She laughed. "You don't golf."

"I can learn," he said, managing to look insulted.

"Do you need a caddy?"

"No!" he growled. "You're going to remain at *Pinnacle* and become the editor you're capable of being," he said in a quieter tone. "Nick is going to make that possible for you."

She glanced at Nicholas who was talking to Asia Beaumont, one of two female editors for the magazine. Asia, as exotic as her mellifluous name, stunning in a blood-red silk wrap dress, had Nicholas's full attention when he smiled down into her black, doe-shaped eyes. As if he could feel the heat of Dyana's gaze boring into his back, he turned and caught her staring. The seconds stretched into a minute as their eyes were locked in a soporific trance. He smiled at Asia and excused himself.

Why couldn't he be brilliant, but short, fat and ugly, she thought when he headed toward her. Nicholas Bradshaw reminded her that she was a woman with all of the normal reactions a woman should feel toward an attractive man. It was as if she'd been frozen for six years and had just begun to thaw.

The light gray jacket was molded to a set of broad shoulders, tapering at the waist. He pulled down the French cuffs to his shirt, revealing a pair of gold monogrammed cuff links. "I'll see you home whenever you're ready."

She was more than ready. Streaks of yellow and orange crisscrossed the sky over the Hudson River, casting darkening shadows on the Jersey shore. Dusk was rapidly descending on the island of Manhattan. The insistent laughter, chatter and nibbling on hors d'oeuvres, washed down with two glasses of wine, had left her drained and weary. "I'm ready."

People were standing around the apartment in small groups as she and Nicholas made their good-byes. She couldn't protest when he held her hand firmly to lead her down the hall to the elevator. "How many glasses of wine did you have?" he asked when she closed her eyes.

"Two."

"You'd be a cheap date, Dyana Randolph."

"A cheaper drunk," she said, leaning against the wall of the elevator when the doors closed, ignoring the grin on his handsome face.

His fingers closed across her smaller hand, tucking it into the bend of his arm. "A little fresh air should clear your head," he suggested.

She nodded, wondering how much of a cure the hot, humid June weather would be.

There was little pedestrian traffic along Riverside Drive. Nicholas adjusted his longer legs to her shorter stride, making it seem like a leisurely stroll along the park. Stately prewar buildings facing the river, rows of prolific trees and the gentle lapping of water against the shore made for a romantic setting. Dyana fought the urge to lean against the solid frame of the tall man beside her and give in to the longing of having a young man hold her and make her feel desirable. It had been too long since she'd been kissed. Kissed with passion.

The clicking of her heels on the cobblestone path was unusually loud, alternating with the slapping of rotating tires on the roadway. There was an occasional bark from a dog and the sonorous roar from a passing aircraft. It all seemed eerie that this residential avenue of Manhattan was so different from many other sections of the city. At dusk, it appeared to settle down and go to sleep while others were awake, alive with bright lights and noise.

Nicholas stopped next to a light gray Corvette, leaning over to unlock the door. He seated her, then walked around to the driver's side. He waited until she'd slipped her belt over her chest and waist before turning on the ignition and putting the sports car into gear.

Leaning back against the black leather seat, she closed her tired, aching eyes. "Go north up the drive until One Hundred Forty-fifth, then make a right on Convent Avenue."

Nicholas turned on the headlights and pulled away from the curb in one swift, powerful motion. The slender woman next to him was intriguing. He could understand Doug Jenkins's feeling of rejection; no man wanted to hear the sharp edge which crept into her voice without warning or have her look through him as if he had ceased to exist.

Now Michael Dalton was another matter. With Michael she was soft, giving and totally feminine. "Where did you pick up your entertaining skills, Dyana?" he asked, wanting to know more about her.

"From Randy's Rib Rack," she murmured hoarsely.

He took a quick glance at her face. "From where?"

She smiled, not opening her eyes. "My father has a catering business in Philadelphia," she explained. "He began in a tiny store selling the best barbecued ribs and chicken in North Philly. The lines were out of the door and around the corner on Friday and Saturday nights during the summer when it was too hot to cook."

"Go on," he urged.

She opened her eyes, smiling. "It was the sauce. The thick, dark red sauce is Daddy's secret. He refuses to tell my mother because he's afraid she would disclose his 'secret' when gossiping with friends or relatives. I've accused him of being a sexist when he says women gossip too much, but he won't budge."

"What else does he prepare?"

"All the trimmings: greens, potato salad, cole slaw, biscuits, black-eyed peas and cornbread. He expanded after a couple of years, but was forced to relocate when an urban renewal plan rezoned the area to include the block for middle-income residential structures."

Nicholas stopped for a red light. Turning his head, he studied her intently. "Was Randy's Rib Rack forced to go out of business?"

"No. He now operates out of a mini-mall where everything is modern and fancy, but the food is still as it was when he first went into business in a twenty-by-twenty storefront. He and my mother cater weddings, sweet sixteen parties and office parties."

"Are the lines still around the corner on Friday and Saturday nights?"

Her laugh was light and tinkling in the close confines of the car. "No. The mall closes down at seven and most people get there around five or six to carry out multiple orders."

His low, rumbling laughter joined hers. "I think I prefer the old neighborhood."

"So would my father," she agreed. She'd just pulled her eyes away from his strong profile when a flash of bright light blinded her. "Nicholas!" she screamed once before hearing the explosion and feeling the stabbing pain along her right side. She continued to scream his name, reaching out in the darkness for something to hold on to.

TWO

"Don't move, Dyana!"

"I . . . I can't move," she moaned above the sound of sirens. Splinters of red and white color pierced her tightly closed lids. Any motion drove the shredlike needles deeper into her arm.

"It's all right, darling. You're going to be all right," Nicholas repeated over and over. He supported her head against his shoulder as he unbuckled her seat belt.

His soothing voice and gentle hands helped stem the spiraling panic shaking her limbs. She opened her eyes to see the windshield swaying from its frame like a silvery gossamer web. She mumbled a prayer under her breath; she was alive. She had seen the speeding car before Nicholas did and still it had been too late to avoid the collision.

"Hey, man, do you need a witness? I saw the whole thing. That dude must have been doing a good ninety before he creamed you and . . ."

The dying wail of a siren drowned out the bystander's statement as a police car pulled alongside the battered Corvette. The police officer quickly assessed the accident and radioed for an ambulance while his partner took charge to control the quickly gathering crowd of onlookers. "Let's go, folks. Step back."

The flashing lights atop the approaching squad cars cast eerie shadows on the angles and planes of Nicholas's face. Fear, stark and vivid lined his forehead and tightened his mouth, but she didn't see it because she lay against his chest, swallowing back her own. She'd screamed his name, moaned, then bit her lower lip to keep from shaming herself. The only time she'd said his name, it was in fear, and the sound of it continued to reverberate in her head.

"I saw the whole thing, officer," the young man volunteered, gesturing wildly.

The youthful policeman shot him a questioning look. "Sure, pal. Hang around and I'll get an eyewitness statement from you." He leaned through the opened window. "How is she?" he asked Nicholas.

"I'm still alive," Dyana mumbled against the hardness of his chest.

Nicholas smiled in spite of the seriousness of the circumstances. "She says she's alive."

Dyana lay on the stretcher, gritting her teeth as glass was extracted from her arm and the tiny cuts covered with a liquid which set the sensitive flesh afire.

"You're a lucky young woman, Mrs. Bradshaw."

She turned her head slowly to stare at the doctor. "What did you say?"

He squeezed her bare shoulder under the sheet. "I said, you're lucky." He reached up to rub the back of his neck in a gesture which mirrored the fatigue an intern experiences when working the emergency room in a large city hospital. Exhaustion clouded compassionate gray eyes. "I could've spent the last forty minutes picking pieces of glass out of your face instead of your arm." He nodded to a nurse. "Miss Benson will help you into your clothes while I talk to your husband. I want you to stay off your feet until the swelling in your right leg disappears. Then you'll still have to exercise a bit of caution. Try not to push yourself too quickly, Mrs. Bradshaw."

Her movements were stiff and mechanical when she allowed the nurse to help her dress. No broken bones; no concussion. Just minor cuts on her arm where slivers of glass pierced the sleeve of her jacket and a severely bruised right knee and leg. What was it the doctor called her? Mrs. Bradshaw? Why had Nicholas registered her as Dyana Bradshaw instead of Dyana Randolph? She didn't have to wait for an answer.

Nicholas cradled her gently in a loose embrace after he'd carried her to the waiting taxi. "I couldn't take the risk that if you needed surgery I'd have to wait for a relative to sign the papers granting permission. As it was, I couldn't remember your last name. I was scared, Dyana," he confessed. "I should've seen that clown speeding like a bat out of hell."

"You couldn't see him," she slurred, her voice showing the effects of the painkiller she'd been given.

"I still should've been more alert," he insisted, lowering his chin to the top of her head.

Her right hand moved up his chest and curled around his neck. The steady pounding of his heart drummed rhythmically against her ear. He felt warm, strong, and her mouth curved in the beginnings of a smile as her eyelids fluttered closed. "It's not your fault, Nicholas," she mumbled dream-like.

The soft sound of breathing and the gentle rising and falling of her chest indicated she'd retreated into darkness; darkness which swept her away to where she couldn't know of Nicholas's fear; fear as real as what he'd experienced when photographing the aftermath of battles in Southeast Asia.

The entire episode could've been completely erased from her memory if it had not been for the pain. She tried pulling up to support her back against the pillows and failed; moaning softly, she threw back the sheet to stare at the swollen mass of what should've been her right leg. The knee was twice its normal size and the circumference of her calf was as large as her thigh. Even her toes resembled brown breakfast sausage links. How was she to put a shoe on? Walk? Raising her arm, she noted the orange-tinged solution on the tiny cuts on her forearm.

She ran her left hand through the tangled mass of hair falling over her forehead, remembering Nicholas, the accident and the hospital. "Susie." She swallowed and fell back against the pillows. Her aunt's name came out in a croaking sound. She massaged her throat. Had she injured her throat as well as her leg? She heard her aunt's footsteps and humming outside of the door. "Susie," she croaked again.

She had almost given up when the door opened and a round smiling face, belonging to an equally round body, waddled into the bedroom. "Well, well, well. Just you look at who finally woke up."

Dyana stared up at the pattern of the wallpaper on the ceiling. "What happened to my voice?"

Susan Randolph sat down heavily on the rocker beside the bed and raised the sheet to examine her niece's leg. She pushed her glasses up on her nose. "I wouldn't worry too much about your voice, child. It's this leg that has me worried." She lowered the sheet. "It's gonna be a while before you'll be able to walk in those pointy toed shoes you like to priss around in."

She knew about her leg. "What's wrong with my throat?" Dyana stared at the face so much like her own. Thirty years and fifty pounds and a sprinkling of gray was all that distinguished aunt from niece.

Susie busied herself straightening the bed covers. "That young man who brought you home . . ."

"What about him?" she questioned when her aunt didn't finish the statement.

"Well, it seems as if you didn't want him to leave you," she said slowly, watching the brown eyes grow larger in astonishment.

"What!" She tried getting up, but the spasm of pain quickly reminded her that she'd become an invalid.

Susie ran the hem of her apron over the top of the bedside table, brushing away a layer of nonexistent dust. "It probably was shock and the drugs the doctor gave you in the hospital. Well . . . you started to cry when he left you and . . ."

"And what?" she squeaked in embarrassment.

"He stayed until you cried yourself to sleep."

She rolled over on her side, unmindful of the pain and

covering her face with a forearm. How could she have acted like a complete idiot? It would've been better if she had become the hysterical female instead of becoming a fool, even if she couldn't remember being one. "What did he say?"

Susie returned to the bed, pulling Dyana against her breasts. "He was so gentle, Dee. He held you a long time after you'd fallen asleep. He didn't say so, but I think he blamed himself for your getting hurt."

Dyana wound her arms around her aunt's neck. The soft clean fragrance of lilac filled her nostrils. For as long as she could remember, Susan Randolph always wore that cologne. Aunt Susie understood her better than her parents or brothers. She proudly exclaimed that they were so much alike—in looks and in temperament. Both of them were free spirits and it would take an exceptional man to capture their hearts.

"There was no way he could have avoided being hit."

Susie eased her back to the pillows, pulling the sheet up over her shoulders. "It's over and thank God no one was seriously injured." She kissed her forehead. "Your Nicholas probably needed something to pull his nerves together before he left here last night."

Dyana sat up again. "His car. How did he get home?"

Susie pushed her down. "Don't worry, child. The man made it home. He called less than an hour ago to find out how you were feeling. I told him you were still asleep and that I would let you know he called." She picked up a pink sponge roller which had slipped from a fat curl at the back of her head. "For a couple of strangers, you two sure worry a bit much about each other." She redid the roller. "I'll bring you some food, then I'll help you get washed and dressed. Can't have you laying around like somebody sick."

She couldn't believe it. Crying—no, weeping would've been a more appropriate term. Weeping like a vapid female and imploring him not to leave her; and he'd stayed.

The door opened. "What happened to you, girlfriend? Your aunt tells me you'll be bedridden for a while?"

Dyana gave her best friend and neighbor a weak grin. "Come take a look at this leg, Livvy. Tell me if you've ever seen anything like it," she was able to say glibly.

Livvy's jaw dropped when Dyana pulled back the sheet to reveal her injured limb. Livvy pushed her glasses up on her nose in an unconscious gesture and sank down slowly on the edge of the bed. She held up her hand. "Wait, don't tell me. You went dancing and William 'The Refrigerator' Perry stepped on your foot."

Dyana grimaced. "Very funny, Miss Patterson."

Livvy chewed a fingernail. "No—I know now. You were attacked by a gang of karate experts and you were forced to use your feet to break boards and bricks to subdue them."

Dyana snapped the sheet over her leg with a vicious flick of the wrist. "Get out!"

Livvy dissolved into a paroxysm of laughter. "I'm sorry," she sputtered. "Honest," she cried, tears staining her face.

Dyana sank down to the pillows, smiling. Olivia Patterson was as comforting as an old shoe. She refused to take life seriously. Her profession as a child psychologist forced her to laugh at the less grave side of daily life. She'd moved into the adjoining apartment eighteen months before, depressed after the breakup of her five-year marriage to a fellow psychologist. It had taken her only two months to pull herself out of her dark mood before she began doing all of the things she had missed: traveling, purchasing outrageously expensive clothes and having braces put on her teeth to improve an overbite. Now, at the age of thirty-three, Dr. Olivia Patterson was enjoying life.

Dyana had appreciated her friend's efforts to fix her up with dates and they had occasionally double dated. Livvy, three inches taller than her own five feet four inches, appeared shorter because of her voluptuous figure. Most men took one quick look at the endowed figure and their glands began to shift into overdrive. Some of them took the time to look past her full hips to appreciate her bubbly, glowing personality.

"I was in an auto accident," she volunteered when Livvy recovered.

"When?"

"Last night."

"What happened?" Livvy asked, exhibiting a measure of seriousness for the first time.

"A nut was doing about eighty-five when he tried making a left at One Forty-fifth and Riverside. Apparently he spun out of control and hit our car, catching the right side when Nicholas was about to make a turn."

"Nicholas who?" Her eyes narrowed in suspicion in a café-au-lait brown face behind tinted lenses with oval red frames.

Now it was Dyana's turn to smile. Any mention of a man was top priority for Livvy. She'd almost given up on Dyana's dating. "Nicholas Bradshaw."

"Mercy me," she sighed, raising her eyebrows. "You and Nicholas Bradshaw," she replied in awe. "Wonders never cease." She laid a slender hand on Dyana's forehead. "What, no fever? Being in the same car as Nicholas Bradshaw didn't raise your blood pressure, Miss Randolph?"

"Sitting next to Nicholas Bradshaw didn't affect me as much as nearly being demolished in his tiny car."

Livvy moved over to sit in the rocker. "I don't believe you, Dyana. You lay there so composed as if you have no nerve endings or emotions. You get the chance to be with the most beautiful black man in the world and . . ." She snapped her fingers. "Nothing. I don't think I'd make it through the day."

Dyana shrugged slender shoulders. "Once you recover from his looks, he's only another man. No more, no less."

Livvy leaned forward, frowning. "He's just another man because you have a tired old man who's fulfilling your needs, Dyana. Think about it, girlfriend. Your relationship with Michael Dalton is abnormal. He's more than twice your age, and he can't offer you anything except his company and money."

Dyana looked at her friend with a baleful expression. "Michael is my friend and we enjoy each other's company. Besides, we have similar interests."

Livvy couldn't help smiling. "Sure, things comatose people enjoy. But I must say the man knows how to throw a party." She reached over to take Dyana's hand and squeezed it tightly. "You're a young, beautiful, vibrant woman and you're wasting your looks and talent on a man who's replacing your father."

Dyana returned the smile, unable to take offense at Livvy's remarks. "Are you Livvy or are you Dr. Patterson this morning?"

Livvy looked contrite. "You're not my patient, Dyana. To you I'll always be your friend."

She stared at Livvy and nodded. "And it's not often someone can find a friend like you. Thanks for the advice, but I'm going to have to get used to not having Michael as a shield in another month. With his retirement, we won't be quite so available for each other."

"Can you imagine the gossip when you and Nicholas Bradshaw attend a social event together?"

"Don't even think it," she warned. "I can't see myself starting over with Nicholas. There will be no way I'll be able to get away with trying to convince people that he and I are not having an affair. Michael, maybe. Nicholas, never!"

"It would be worth it."

"Worth what?"

"Carrying on with Nicholas Bradshaw."

Susie entered the bedroom, carrying a tray filled with a variety of tantalizing smells. "I guess you're going to hang around," she mumbled to Livvy.

"Of course, Aunt Susie," Livvy returned.

"When are you going to learn how to cook?" Susie grumbled, placing the tray on a small table. "No wonder your husband left you. It was either leaving or dying of ptomaine."

Livvy tried to look insulted. "My talents lie elsewhere and the kitchen isn't one of them."

"Livvy's right," Dyana said, coming to her friend's aid and

hoping to avoid a confrontation between her aunt and neighbor. "Today's modern woman isn't forced to cook or keep house to hold on to a husband."

"You, Dyana Randolph, stay out of this! You can cook, she can't. And you, Miss Patterson, if you could cook as well as you can talk, you'd be doing the world some good. I bet you can talk life into the dead."

Livvy reached for a fluffy biscuit. "If you're looking for a fight this morning, forget it, Aunt Susie. I'm much too hungry to pretend I'm insulted."

A loud sucking of teeth told Livvy exactly what Susie thought of her as she rolled her eyes in a threatening manner. "I've filled the tub with water for your bath, Dee. As soon as you and that freeloader finish eating, we'll help you to the bathroom."

Susie and Livvy couldn't get along together for more than five minutes. They were too much alike, saying exactly what was on their minds, and Dyana loved them both for their straightforward honesty. Some of the words cut to the quick, but it was always the truth.

Unlike her parents and brothers who tended to shield her from the unpleasantries of life, Susie and Livvy shocked her with their candor. Growing up with four brothers was akin to solitary confinement. As an adolescent, boys avoided her like the plague after encountering the glowering, menacing glares from the Randolph brothers. It had taken years before she realized she wasn't physically repulsive when she couldn't get a date, and she had paid for the inexperience when she found herself involved with a man who overwhelmed her with his worldliness.

She forgot her childhood when biting into a slice of delicately broiled pink ham. The accompanying onion omelet and light buttery biscuits were common fare for a Saturday morning brunch.

"I really would've preferred grits and onion gravy this morning, Aunt Susie," Livvy said, wiping away a trace of strawberry jelly from her mouth.

"Wrong day, Livvy. We normally have grits on Sunday," Dyana remarked.

"Can't you pretend it's Sunday, Aunt Susie? You know I don't eat with you on Sundays."

"Every day should be Sunday," Susie replied sweetly. "And stop calling me your aunt. I have a parrot who talks too much and a niece who refuses to get married. What do I need with another unmarried niece who doesn't know when to stop talking?"

Livvy poured steaming coffee into thick white mugs, handing one to Dyana. "She really loves me, Dyana."

Dyana nodded in agreement. "She loves me, too."

"I'll get it," Livvy volunteered when the doorbell chimed throughout the apartment. She set her tray on the table in the corner of the bedroom Susie had decorated with the cheerful gingham of a typical country French fabric.

Susie put on her glasses, hanging from a gold chain around her neck, to concentrate on measuring sugar into her coffee. "She's becoming impossible. Next she'll ask me to adopt her."

Livvy returned to the bedroom, a hand clutching her chest. "Dyana . . . Dyana," she sputtered weakly. "He's here."

"Who?" She sounded like a hoarse owl.

Livvy closed the door, wet-look curls shaking furiously, then spun around to peer through the crack. "Nicholas Bradshaw!"

"Silly woman," Susie grumbled, pushing herself out of the rocker. "I bet you left him standing in the middle of the living room. Probably didn't invite him to sit because for once your mouth was open catching flies instead of trying to show him the good manners your mother brought you up with."

Dyana wanted to sink down under the sheet and hide. How was she to see him with her hair sticking out all over her head and dressed in a skimpy nightgown?

"Did you know he was coming?" she asked her aunt.

"Sure did," Susie confessed, waddling quickly across the

room. "That's why I wanted you dressed before he got here."

"Help me," Dyana squeaked to a mute Livvy.

Food forgotten, Livvy helped her out of the bed and she limped to the bathroom where the tub had been filled with bath crystals in her favorite scent. At another time she would've spent a leisurely half hour in the tub, but this morning she set a record when she bathed, brushed her teeth and dressed all within the half hour. Susie had left an aluminum cane on the doorknob to help her when she tried standing unaided. The cane was a reminder of the time her aunt had broken her big toe when she dropped a can of stewed tomatoes on her foot. Susie looked upon stewed tomatoes as a bad omen and refused to prepare some of her favorite dishes which called for the sauce; but to Dyana the cane was a boon, for she doubted whether she would've been able to walk without it.

Whatever curl was left in her hair was brushed up in a tight knot atop her head and secured with pins. She examined her unmade face and frowned. Without makeup she appeared no older than some of the girls who attended a nearby high school.

She heard his distinctive deep voice before she hobbled into the living room. She tightened her grip on the handle of the cane when she saw him. No wonder Livvy was at a loss for words. She was unable to believe a man could look so incredibly virile in a shirt and a pair of slacks. A short-sleeve dark green cotton knit shirt was molded to his body like skin while a pair of khaki slacks emphasized a slim, muscled physique. Dark brown loafers and socks completed his casual attire.

His gaze missed her face as they went to the injured leg. A midi-length denim skirt with a dropped yoke in front and back failed to hide the swelling in her ankle and toes. She wiggled bare toes under his slow perusal.

He stood up to assist her, his right arm circling her waist. "How are you feeling?" he asked, pulling her against his thigh.

"Better," she said in a heavy whisper. She gave in to the uncontrollable urge to lean against him. It was what she'd felt the day before. His fingers tightened, molding her length to his. It seemed natural and right. Her senses were filled with his strength, smell and masculine beauty. The top of her head reached his shoulder and she felt tiny without her heels.

Susie and Livvy exchanged glances when Nicholas settled Dyana in a smoky-blue velvet chair with a matching ottoman. Their eyes followed his hands when he gently raised her foot to place it on the ottoman.

"The flowers on the table are from Mr. Bradshaw, Dee," Susie said when she was comfortably seated.

"And the box of chocolates," Livvy chimed in.

"Thank you, Nicholas. They're beautiful," she replied, her voice fading. A large crystal vase held a profusion of long-stemmed blood-red roses nestled in ferns and baby's breath. The large royal blue-and-silver box contained the exquisite chocolates of Perugina.

Nicholas sat on a burgundy damask sofa, stretching long legs out in front of him. "Beautiful flowers for a beautiful lady."

She looked away, grateful she could blame her silence on injured vocal cords. What was it about Nicholas, other than his looks, which made her react like a shy adolescent? Her pulse raced a little faster, her heart leaped and fluttered and she was unable to form her thoughts to give him a mature response. Was she in awe of his name and reputation? Or was it because she'd lowered her resistance?

"Was there much damage to your car, Mr. Bradshaw?" Susie questioned.

"Please call me Nicholas," he insisted. "The front end sustained quite a bit of damage, but the mechanic should be able to restore it to its original state, Mrs. Randolph."

Susie puffed up her chest like a ruffled bird. "It's Miss Susie Randolph, Nicholas. Dyana happens to be my niece, not my daughter." She pointed to a sepia-colored photograph on the mantel over the fireplace. "Dee looks like my mother.

When she was a little girl she had her Grandma Dinah's reddish hair. Now that she's older, there's hardly a trace."

Nicholas looked at the photograph, then at the dark hair piled on Dyana's head, remembering the shimmering auburn curls from the day before. "It's incredible how much the three of you look alike, Susie. I'm certain people mistake you and Dyana for mother and daughter."

Susie's eyes sparkled when she was able to engage in her favorite topic: family history. "Dee's father is my twin brother." She shot a quick glance at an enraptured Livvy. "Olivia, please bring the coffee and the pie from the kitchen for me. Even though Nicholas says he's eaten, I'm sure he wouldn't want to pass up a slice of Dyana's sweet-potato pie."

Livvy's movements resembled a slug's when she reluctantly left the living room, pulling an oversized yellow shirt down over a pair of skintight jeans. Dyana could almost read her mind: Susie would pay for the ploy.

Nicholas crossed his legs. "We seem to have something in common. My mother is also a twin and my sister has a set of twin girls."

"Do you have any children?" Susie asked, repositioning her slippered feet on a dark red area rug with an intricately woven floral pattern. Dyana wanted to disappear. Her aunt was about to re-create the Inquisition.

"No, I don't," Nicholas replied, seemingly eager to answer her question. "I was married for a short time a while back, but my ex-wife and I didn't stay together long enough to start a family."

"What happened?"

"I accepted an overseas assignment and she was busy trying to establish a singing and acting career here in the States."

Susie shook her head. "Why did you get married?"

"I don't know. It's not as if we loved each other." Even though he'd spoken to Susie, his eyes were fixed on Dyana's face.

"Do you want children?" Susie continued with her questioning.

"I'd love to have a child."

"Only one?"

He smiled, running a hand through his short cropped hair. "Most people begin with one, don't they?"

"Not so with your family or mine," Susie rationalized. "It seems as if we have children in matched sets."

He laughed. "You've got a point."

Dyana breathed a sigh of relief when Livvy returned with the coffee and pie. Instinctively she knew her aunt's next comment would've referred to her and Nicholas and the odds of them having twins instead of single births; however, a quick look at Nicholas revealed he was charmed by Susie's questions. This Nicholas Bradshaw was nothing like the one she'd read or heard about. Reports indicated he was brash, self-centered and aloof. The man sitting in her living room was nothing like his image.

And for the first time since meeting him, she noticed things she hadn't before: his hair wasn't totally black; there was a liberal sprinkling of gray in the dark curls and his eyes changed from dark green to a luminous smoky gray depending upon his mood. His mood was light and so were his eyes.

Livvy placed a gleaming silver serving tray on an eighteenth-century-style ball and claw table of cherry hardwood. The translucent china gleamed under the muted light of an overhead brass chandelier.

"Milk and sugar, Nicholas?" Livvy purred like a satisfied feline. Dr. Olivia Patterson had become the seducer and she was rewarded with a wide grin from Nicholas.

"Just milk, please." He took the silver coffeepot from Livvy and poured coffee into a fragile cup. "How would you like yours, Dyana?"

"Milk and one sugar," she rasped. Again she was unbalanced by his offer to serve her and she wondered what had happened between him and his wife to dissolve their marriage.

There was only the sound of rattling china cups and sterling forks against silver-gilded-edged plates while generous slices of pie were consumed. Susie didn't have to tell Livvy that she wanted her best china and silverware when serving company. She prided herself on the magnificent furnishings in her brownstone apartment. Eighteenth-century designs were abundant through the living and dining rooms. A ball and claw chair was covered with a Cluny tapestry, and needlepoint designs were in evidence on footstools, wall hangings and pillows. Susie had begun sewing as a child and eventually became an accomplished dressmaker with wedding gowns as her speciality. She worked for a bridal manufacturer for twenty-five years, then decided to go into business for herself after purchasing the brownstone building along Harlem's Convent Avenue. She managed to earn enough money to live in relaxed comfort.

Nicholas smiled at Dyana, eyebrows inching up and allowing him to appear boyish. "I'll share the last piece with you."

She registered an expression of pure panic from Livvy. Dyana wanted the last slice, but cognizant of Livvy's lack of culinary skills, decided to decline. "No thanks. Share it with Livvy. Sitting around for the next few days will take its toll if I continue to eat like this."

Livvy cut the remaining portion in half. "Don't believe her. Dyana can eat a pound of french fries and never put on an ounce. She's the only woman I know who never gains weight or gets a pimple. Sometimes I hate her," she added before biting into a piece of creamy pie.

"Eating food like this is sinful," Nicholas admitted. "I'm afraid I have to agree with Dyana. One week in this house and I'd begin to look like a sumo wrestler."

"For a man who spends his day sitting at a desk, you look pretty fit to me," Livvy purred again.

"I work out a lot."

Susie grunted loudly. "Eat Olivia's cooking and you won't have to work out. You'd be so weak you wouldn't be able to raise your head from the pillow in the morning."

"We all have our talents, Aunt Susie," Livvy retorted. "Cooking just happens not to be one of mine."

"Do they always go at each other like that?" Nicholas asked when Susie silently ordered Livvy to the kitchen with her.

"Yes." She stared as he stretched an arm over the back of the sofa. The black hair on his arms made the tanned flesh even darker and the corded muscles in his forearms and wrists gave witness to his working out. There wasn't an ounce of excess fat on his body. "They're quite fond of each other despite their verbal sparring."

Nicholas left the sofa to sit on the ottoman, positioning her foot in his lap. His eyes had deepened to a dark green and she wanted to ease her foot out of his grip but couldn't when his fingers inched up her ankle to the calf. A flush flooded her body and she wanted to pull her white tee shirt away from her moist flesh.

He stared at her, deep lines appearing in his smooth forehead. "I'm sorry, Dyana. I've said it over and over to myself and somehow it doesn't quite sound adequate."

"Then don't say it," she whispered. "It wasn't your fault." She couldn't keep the tremor from surfacing. "How do you think I would've felt if all I got was a fat leg and you were lying in a hospital hooked up to tubes and machines? You were where you were because of me, Nicholas. If you hadn't been driving me home, none of this would've happened."

His incredible mouth curved into a smile. "For a slightly bruised, sexy-sounding woman, you plead a good case, Dyana Randolph."

Her lashes lowered, concealing large golden brown eyes. "Now that we understand each other, I suggest we drop the issue."

"Agreed." He stood and reached down to pick her up. "It's easier talking to you with you sitting next to me," he explained when she gasped in surprise. His fingers curved under her breast and she felt successful when she didn't bury her face in his neck. He settled her on the sofa and retrieved the ottoman for her foot. He sat beside her, again stretching an arm over the sofa. She only had to lean back for his hand to touch her neck. He was close, too close, but she enjoyed his presence. His closeness didn't fill her with the sense of dread which happened whenever she found herself in the company of a young man.

"You're going to be out of work for at least a week," he said ruefully. "If you get bored, call me and I'll bring you something to work on."

"You must have been reading my mind. After two days I go stir crazy if I have nothing to do."

His warm breath fanned her cheek when he turned his head to look down at her. "So Michael has told me."

She wondered what else Michael had told him. That they hadn't been lovers but friends? That she understood his loneliness after losing his wife of twenty-nine years?

"Which one is the youngest, you or your brother?" He pointed to a faded photograph on a side table. It was a picture taken years before when the Randolphs were dressed in their finery for an Easter Sunday service. She and Evan were wearing almost identical white voile hats except for a satin bow in the back of hers.

"Evan is two years younger than I. The oldest is Jesse. He's now a missionary in Senegal." She identified the smiling faces behind the glass when Nicholas picked up the frame. "Next to him is Tom. This one is Walter. That's me on my father's knee and my mother is holding Evan."

He replaced the photograph at the proper angle on the table. "How did you manage to survive four brothers?"

"I didn't. I became a prisoner in my own house. They thought they were spoiling me when they overreacted with their chauvinism."

He laughed, the sound low and unrestrained. "In other words, they scared away the boys who thought their little sister was fair game."

"How did you know?"

He shrugged broad shoulders under the dark green shirt. "I treated my sister the same way."

She stared at him, then burst into laughter, unaware that

the husky sound of her voice sent chills along his spine. She was weaving an invisible spell neither one of them were aware of. His laughter joined hers and when Susie and Livvy returned to the room, they were shocked and jealous that they hadn't been privy to the secret which allowed Dyana to react with such abandon with a man *not* old enough to be her father.

"Listen to this one. *La chaleur d'un baiser fait fondre le coeur le plus froid.*"

"What does that mean, Livvy?"

Livvy squinted and dropped another chocolate candy into her mouth. "It translates into 'the warmth of a kiss can melt the most icy of hearts.' "

"Whose kiss?"

Livvy waved her hand in the air. "Why Nicholas Bradshaw's of course."

Dyana closed her eyes, shutting out her friend's grinning face. "You're obsessed with the man."

"Just about as obsessed as he is with kisses, girlfriend. The man gives you a box of chocolates filled with hazelnuts and wrapped in paper with erotic sayings. Every erotic line dedicated to kisses and what they can do. These Baci are definitely X-rated. This paper reads 'love without kisses, dozes and then falls asleep.' " She looked at a drowsy Dyana. "Just like you."

"They aren't erotic, Livvy. They're sensual," she mumbled under her breath.

"Like Nicholas?"

"Yes, like Nicholas," she sighed before falling off into a deep, dreamless slumber.

Livvy stacked the small waxed papers with expressions printed in blue in Italian, French, German and English in a milk-white candy dish. Dyana had put on a brave facade for hours, enduring the punishing pain in her knee. Livvy finally convinced her to take the pill the hospital had prescribed, silent for once when she noted the name Dyana Bradshaw typed across the label.

THREE

Dyana sat in the backyard, failing to concentrate on the paperback novel in her lap. It wasn't working; the inactivity was beginning to play havoc with her nerves. The weekend was over and already she was grinding her teeth in frustration. Most of the swelling had left her foot to where she was able to put on a shoe, but the knee refused to bend to allow her to move around without the cane.

Michael had come over for dinner on Sunday, bellowing uncontrollably when he saw her leg, and she had to reassure him she would walk again. *When* was the question.

There was another delivery of flowers bearing Nicholas's card with a scrawled message telling her to get well. Two hours later a large plant arrived with a humorous studio card attached from the employees of the magazine and book company. An exquisite bonsai plant from Nicholas on Tuesday reduced her to tears of laughter when Susie said that if she didn't return to work the house would look like a nursery by the end of the month. It was now Wednesday and she refused to guess at what he would send her.

It was his presence, not a plant, which shocked her when Susie escorted him out to where she was sitting under the shade of a large red and white striped umbrella.

"I left a plant inside for you," he said, taking a webbed chair at the table. A pristine white shirt was a startling contrast to his tanned brown skin. He'd rolled back the cuffs and a wine-colored tie hung from an opened collar. He gave her a tired smile. "How are you feeling?"

"I'm bored to death," she confessed, her voice back to its normal tone. "Did you bring me some work to do?"

Nicholas stared at her for a long time. She looked different. Her hair was shiny and curled into a loose ponytail at the back of her head and her bare face was clear with a healthy glow of red-brown color. In spite of her statement that she was bored, her eyes were brilliant with an unnamed excitement. Was she glad to see him?

He focused on the adjustable cane hanging on the back of her chair. "I was going to bring a few articles for you to work on until I received a package in the mail from a friend of mine."

"What kind of a package, Nicholas?" She sat forward in the chair, not caring whether he recognized her joy in seeing him again. She didn't realize how much she'd missed him until she looked up and saw his tall figure striding toward her. The past three days had been spent trying to remember his voice and mannerisms.

Nicholas waited until Dyana filled a glass with cold, frothy lemonade from the pitcher on the table. He took a swallow, watching her as she watched his Adam's apple slide up and down as the icy liquid bathed his throat and quenched his thirst. He studied her thoughtfully for a moment, the glass poised in midair.

"Do you remember hearing the name Carl Murphy?"

She looked away from his strong neck, nodding. "Who hasn't?" What did he expect her to say? The man's face had appeared on the evening news for weeks two years before. It wasn't an everyday occurrence when a member of the President's administration was fired and subsequently investigated by the Senate for his involvement with illegal military sales to a hostile nation. "He was convicted of being a spy."

"This spy happens to be a personal friend, Dyana," he confessed.

"You have nice friends," she said, her voice rising in surprise.

Nicholas ignored her retort. "Carl sent me a manuscript describing everything that happened before, during and after his trial."

"No!" she cried, knowing what was coming next. She closed her eyes when she felt a chill shake her body.

Nicholas leaned closer, his hand going to her shoulder. "He was set up, Dyana," he whispered savagely. "Carl Murphy is no more a traitor to this country than you or I. We used to trade war stories about Vietnam over drinks in a small bar in Washington, D.C."

She reopened her eyes, pulling away from his fingers. Carl Murphy was using Nicholas's influence to get his side of the story to the American people and the world.

"I owe it to Carl's family to see that this book gets published," he insisted.

So this was his secret weapon. Nicholas Bradshaw had managed to capture the confession of one of the most celebrated spies since the Rosenbergs. "Have you read it?"

His shoulders slumped in a weary gesture as he ran a hand over his face, shaking his head. "I haven't had the time. It came into the office just before closing."

"Where is it?"

"I locked it in my desk."

She wanted to feel what he was feeling; believe in what he was believing. "If it's about the charges and his trial, how do you know for sure that he's telling the truth? He may be your friend, but friends have been known to lie."

"That's a chance I'll have to take." His jaw tightened, confirming his stubbornness.

"He's placing your position at *Pinnacle* and your reputation as a journalist at risk by sending it to you," she continued, wanting to be objective. He mumbled a foreign phrase and she stared at him, confused. "What did you say?"

He smiled, softening the harsh lines in his face. "It's German for 'some things are worth risking everything for.'"

This was the Nicholas Bradshaw she'd heard about. This was the opportunist the reporter in the hall had sneered about. Tilting her head at an angle, she gave him a long, penetrating look. "You trust him?"

A wild light blazed in his eyes. "With my life!"

She had to smile. "It looks as if you don't have a choice. You'll have to accept it."

His green eyes clung to hers for a brief moment, surprise clearly written on his face. "Thanks for believing in me, Dyana." He relaxed for the first time since receiving the manuscript. "Carl's not a writer and a lot of editing will have to be done before it can be published."

Her mouth softened into an enchanting smile. "Are you going to give it to Westgate?"

"Only after I extract what I want for *Pinnacle.*"

This was a day for surprises. "You're going to preview it with an excerpt for the magazine?"

Now his eyes were gray. "Four or six weeks before the book is due to hit the bookstores we put out the issue of the magazine . . ."

"Capitalizing on deliberate leaks from our public relations department," she finished for him.

It was his turn to smile. "Michael has taught you well, Miss Randolph."

"Do you have an idea as to the publication date?"

"I'm shooting for November."

"No way! This is June, Nicholas," she argued. "How many pages are you talking about?"

"Over a thousand."

"A thousand!" she repeated. "How are you going to run a magazine and edit a thousand pages in time for a November run?"

"Jim can fill in for me while I'm away."

"Where are you going?" she asked in a small voice.

"It's we, Dyana. It's where are we going."

"Where are *we* going?" Her eyes narrowed in suspicion.

"As soon as your knee can support your weight, you and I are going to New Hampshire where we'll work on this together. I'll edit and you'll type."

"Does Paul know about this?" His expression changed as if she'd struck him across the face.

"Paul Scranton owns the magazine, but I run it, Dyana," he snapped. "Don't ever forget that."

Dictatorial. She met his hostile glare with one of her own. How could she have thought of him as gentle? The tension swelled, igniting the very air between them with an uncontrollable electricity. "Is that all you want to discuss?" she said in disguised fury.

Nicholas rose to his feet. "For today, yes." She blinked and he was gone.

Dyana was still staring at the chair he'd vacated when Susie came out of the house, giving her a wary look. "I guess you've got a bee in your bonnet, too." She glanced up at the cloudless sky. "Want to talk about it?"

"There's nothing to talk about," she mumbled angrily. "Nicholas just reminded me that he was my boss."

Susie picked up a piece of cardboard from the table and began fanning herself. "He being your boss isn't all that's bothering him."

"You tell me what's bothering him."

Susie slapped the cardboard down on the tabletop. "You're a woman, Dyana Randolph. You don't need me to explain what you should already know about men."

"Thanks for the explanation," she called out to her aunt's retreating back. First Nicholas walked away from her and now Susie. Three strikes and you're out, Dyana, she thought.

"Where do you think you're going?"

Dyana ran a large-toothed comb through her crimped hair, fluffing up the bangs. "To work," she said, shaking her head until she achieved the soft fullness she desired. She stared at Susie's frowning face in the reflection of the mirror and applied a soft orange lip gloss, emphasizing the rich red tones in her clear sienna-brown complexion. "Something wrong, Aunt Susie?" She feathered her eyebrows with a small brush.

"What's wrong, Miss Sassy?" Susie folded her hands on her hips. "Only that you're being muleheaded. When the doctors take your leg off you'll spend the rest of your life with only one leg. That cane will become your right leg. Then what do I tell my brother?"

Dyana rose slowly from the chair at the dressing table, grimacing against the tightness in her knee and taking a few measured steps to test it. "Tell him that I'm my father's daughter. He'll know because he always said the Randolphs were part Georgia mule."

"Don't expect to get a seat in the subway," Susie shouted when she hobbled toward the door.

"I don't. I'm taking the bus this morning."

The bus ride was long and uncomfortable, but Dyana didn't care; she was ready to endure anything to alleviate the boredom. She'd stopped eating, sleeping and even trying to read. Susie told her to think of her convalescence as a vacation. To her, a vacation was dancing until dawn, sipping potent tropical concoctions and staring up at ribbons of sun piercing the sweeping fronds of towering palm trees, not dozing under the effects of the tiny white pill which shut out the world around her.

"Welcome back, Dyana."

"Thanks," she managed to mumble at the fast-moving figure.

"Hi, Dyana."

"Hi." What was going on? It was nine o'clock and the employees of *Pinnacle* were scurrying around as if they were trying to beat a deadline. The usual small throng in the lounge was conspicuously absent. She'd been away for only four days and apparently the magazine's operation had undergone a change. She limped down the corridor to the office she shared with another editorial assistant.

"What are you doing here?"

She turned, staring up at the puissant figure standing over her. "I thought I'd save you some money by returning to work, Mr. Bradshaw," she quipped.

"How's that, Miss Randolph?" he asked, his fingers cupping her elbow to steer her toward her office.

She savored the familiar fragrance of his after-shave, grinning. More than work, this was what she'd missed and she hadn't realized it until now; she'd missed Nicholas Bradshaw. "All of the flowers and plants must have put quite a dent in your checkbook."

"You're worth it and more," he returned. "Try not to think about my bank balance, Dyana. I can assure you that it can withstand a few purchases." There was a glint of humor in his eyes as they came to rest on her smiling face. They inched down to the soft flowing fabric of a blouson dress in an orange floral print on white rayon. Elbow-length full sleeves and hip smocking hid the slim curves of her body. Low white leather flats were in deference to her injured leg. "Are you ready for our assignment?"

"Mr. Bradshaw, Mr. Scranton is waiting for you," came the receptionist's page throughout the office.

"Come with me, Dyana," Nicholas ordered.

She had no choice but to follow his strong lead as he led her through the connecting offices of *Pinnacle* and Westgate Publishing.

Again she heard the welcome back and the good morning Mr. Bradshaw as she followed Nicholas. Paul Scranton's secretary gave them a friendly smile. "Good morning, Nicholas. Paul is waiting for you. Hope you're feeling better, Dyana."

"Much better, thank you," she said.

Nicholas opened the door, allowing her to precede him into a spacious room with floor-to-ceiling windows along three of the four walls. If an office expressed its occupant's taste, Paul Scranton's revealed his hobby of collecting. Glass-enclosed cabinets displayed a profusion of antique clocks and snuffboxes.

Paul glanced up when they entered, rising to his feet. "Dyana, Bradshaw," he acknowledged with a warm greeting. He waited until Nicholas seated her in a leather lounge chair in front of the massive rosewood desk before retaking his own. "What's so important that I had to terminate my trip to come back to New York, Bradshaw?"

She stared at Nicholas's bold profile. The set of his strong jaw indicated his stubborn streak. "Carl Murphy sent me his story," he said quietly.

Paul tensed, then his dark blue eyes glittered with delight.

The recently divorced, wealthy publisher had become the latest prey for the single women at the company, each vying for his attention. Unfortunately, what most of them didn't know was that Paul was still very much in love with his ex-wife and continued to date her despite their divorce. His tall, trim physique and graying hair prompted most women to take a second look when he entered a room, and Dyana found herself comparing him to Nicholas and concluding he didn't come close.

"Well I'll be a horny toad," he rasped. "Who else knows that you have it?"

Nicholas folded his arms over his chest, the sleeves of his navy blazer tightening around his biceps. "Only the three of us and Michael."

"We're going to take it, Bradshaw."

"I assume you have a good idea as to what it contains, don't you?" Nicholas questioned.

"Yes, I do," Paul replied slowly.

"Even though we have a new administration," Nicholas continued, "there are people in positions of power Carl will be certain to mention. Are you willing to risk a libel suit by publishing it?"

The bright light dimmed in Paul's eyes. A pregnant silence hung heavily in the office and Dyana felt as if her heart could be heard pounding outside of her chest as it resounded loudly in her ears. She had gotten over her initial fear of Nicholas's friendship with a known spy when she realized she was being presented with the opportunity of becoming involved with a history-making event; the book was certain to become a best-seller and also unlock a closet filled with secrets known only by a privileged few.

"Damn, Bradshaw! Whatever happened to the first amendment? I'm willing to go with it!"

A tiny cry of triumph escaped her parted lips when she looked from one man to the other. Nicholas shot her a dazzling smile and winked.

Leaning back, he crossed his left leg over the right. Suddenly his expression was grim. "I'll give it to you, but not without certain concessions."

"What concessions?" Paul barked.

"It's yours only after *Pinnacle* gets it and we negotiate an advance I feel is adequate for Murphy's wife."

"What do you mean, Bradshaw?" Paul asked in a brusque tone.

Dyana held her breath. She knew what was coming next. "I'm going to read it and extract what I want from it for the magazine before you get it; and I want an advance in excess of five hundred thousand for Ronnie Murphy."

Paul's face darkened in rage. "Now, just you wait a minute . . ."

"No, *you* wait," Nicholas said, his voice low and cutting. How different he was from Michael. Michael wasn't adverse to shouting his orders, while Nicholas achieved the same results by not raising his voice above its normal tone.

"Forget it!"

Nicholas's eyes glittered like cold hard stones. "You're a fool, Paul," he almost growled. "You hired me with the stipulation that I run the magazine and now you're changing in midstream. *Pinnacle* will never attain the readership it once claimed unless you permit me complete autonomy. You want the manuscript for Westgate, but on your terms. It's not going to happen because Carl Murphy is my contact, not yours. And in case your memory still fails you, I'd like to remind you that *Pinnacle* has not been seeing the profits Westgate has been enjoying these past few years. Permit me to extract it or I'll peddle it to Random."

Paul Scranton recognized the strengths he admired when he had first met Nicholas Bradshaw years before; and it was these strengths and his honesty which made him want him as the editor for his magazine. "When can I have it?" he asked, sounding like a spoiled child.

"Give me two weeks. If I can get it to you sooner I will. I've made arrangements for Dyana and myself to spend the next week or two in New Hampshire at a friend's inn where we'll have the privacy to work on the editing and typing."

Paul laced his fingers behind his head. "You were so certain I would give in that you made arrangements in advance?" he questioned.

"You had no other choice," Nicholas replied without a hint of smugness. "Carl has allowed me total responsibility to edit where I feel it is feasible. He may have to spend the rest of his life behind bars, but I intend to see that his wife and children will live with a measure of financial security for the remainder of theirs. If we can get it into the October issue, there should be no reason why you can't have the first edition ready for the Christmas season."

Paul ran his fingers through mixed-gray hair. "I thought your October issue had been set up already."

Nicholas gave him a mocking grin. "It has. But for something like this, we'll make certain allowances."

"Okay, Bradshaw," Paul conceded. "Get it to me before the end of the month and I'll make sure it hits the stands by Thanksgiving and Murphy's wife gets the advance in excess of the five hundred thousand."

"When are we going to begin this project?" she asked Nicholas as she limped back to the magazine offices.

Tiny lines deepened around his eyes when he smiled down at her. "How about today? You seem a little slow, but you're managing to get around without your cane."

She stumbled, but he caught her. His strong fingers tightened on her upper arms and she nodded when regaining her balance. "Thank you." Was she ready to spend a week, maybe two, with Nicholas Bradshaw? Could she trust herself not to give in to the feelings which surfaced without warning? "What time do you want to leave?"

Nicholas gave her a long, searching look. Dyana Randolph was good, very good when it came to hiding what she was feeling. Nothing about her revealed the excitement she was experiencing when she thought of her involvement with what was certain to become the book of the year. "Be ready to leave around noon."

"You'll make it, Dyana," Michael reassured her. "Pay close attention to his style and in no time you'll understand what makes him tick."

She closed her eyes and chewed her lower lip. "It's not Nicholas I'm worried about."

Michael pulled at the hair over his left ear. "If it's not Nicholas then it must be Dyana. Right?"

Reopening her eyes, she nodded. "I'm afraid of myself and what I feel whenever I'm around him."

Michael grasped her hands and pulled her to his chest. "That's because you've hung around this old man too long when you should've been dating the young guys: young men who remind you that you're a young woman when they hold you and kiss you until you're breathless."

"Why you're a romantic, Michael Dalton," she exclaimed when seeing his soulful eyes soften with the memories. Somewhere along the way she'd forgotten Michael had married his childhood sweetheart and remained married for twenty-nine years until his beloved Martha died in her sleep one night nearly ten years before. The loss left Michael cold and withdrawn. The magazine staff endured his explosive temper and it wasn't until his secretary walked out and Dyana was recruited from the typing pool to fill in did anyone attempt to draw a comfortable breath when encountering the editor.

Dyana couldn't believe the man with the somber dark eyes in a round cocoa-brown face could scare even the most liberated woman out of her position. With her he never screamed or exhibited his famous temper tantrums and within a month they worked as smoothly as if they had been together for years. And because they functioned so well together, rumors began circulating that she and Michael were having an affair.

"I'm not so old I don't remember what love feels like," he laughed.

She pulled back, staring at the face only inches from her own. "You're not an old man, Michael. I do wish you would stop saying that. I always knew you were special, but never realized how much until of late. Knowing I won't see you frightens me." Her fingers caressed his smooth cheek. "You've been more than a friend, Michael, and I'd always hoped you would become a part of my family."

Michael touched the softness of her hair. "I'm too old for you, child," he protested, misunderstanding her statement.

She pulled her hands out of his loose grip. "Nonsense. You're everything a woman could ever hope for in a husband. You're kind, gentle, intelligent . . ."

"And too old," he repeated, interrupting her. "I have no intention of marrying again," he insisted. "But there's no reason why we can't remain friends even after I leave. Do you think I would give up enjoying Sunday dinner with you and your aunt? It's the only decent meal I have all week." He recaptured her hands. "Promise me you'll find someone your own age and look forward to settling down to raise a family."

"I'm not going to promise you anything of the sort," she retorted softly. She felt Michael's hands tighten and she turned to find Nicholas standing in the doorway watching the interchange. Seeing the frowning expression on his face, she wondered how much of the conversation he had overheard. She didn't have to wonder about how much had been seen as Michael continued to hold her hands between his. When their eyes met, she was uncertain as to what she had seen in the mirrors of Nicholas's soul. Was it anger or was it revulsion?

"Dyana tells me you're going to take her away from me for a week or two," Michael said solemnly.

Don't say that, she thought. Don't make it sound worse than it is. "He's promised me that he'll keep Susie company on Sunday afternoon. She hates to eat alone after she returns from church," she tried explaining, the excuse sounding lame even to herself.

Nicholas's mouth tightened in a gesture she'd come to recognize as annoyance. "You're going to have to help Jim," he said to Michael. "We may not be back in time before everything is set to go."

Michael released Dyana, pushing her toward Nicholas. "Don't worry, Nick. You've done more in a week than Jim or I could do in two. Everything is under control. Take Dyana and get out of here. We need that manuscript."

Susie waved a finger under Nicholas's nose. "You'd better drive careful or I'll make you sorry you ever laid eyes on that girl. No speeding or hot roddin', do you hear me, son?"

"Yes ma'am," he answered, his face solemn.

Susie settled the half-moon glasses on the end of her nose and sat down to work on the intricate stitches as she sewed seeded pearls onto the bodice of a white satin gown.

"Are you finished with the lecture, Aunt Susie?"

Susie didn't bother to look up. "Yeah, I'm finished. Get goin' will you."

Dyana leaned over to kiss her aunt's cheek. "I'll call you when we arrive," she promised, winding her arms around her neck. "I love you," she whispered.

Susie put down her sewing to return the embrace. Tears misted the golden eyes. "I love you too, baby. Come on, I'll walk you to the door."

A loud squawking came from the pantry as they passed the kitchen. "Feed me. Feed me."

"You're not worth what it costs to feed you, George!" Susie shouted at the brightly colored green and blue parrot sitting in a cage.

"I love Michael," George shrieked, flapping its wings. "Feed, Michael."

"Your bird appears to have an identity problem," Nicholas said. "Is he George or Michael?"

"He's going to be one plucked bird if he doesn't stop talking. Hush, George, or I'll put the cover on you."

"Help! Help! Help me; feed me. Michael!"

"Your aunt doesn't trust my driving instincts," Nicholas remarked when he maneuvered the four-wheeler north on the Hudson River Drive.

Dyana settled back against the seat, smiling. "Susie likes to fuss. She's not happy until she has someone to fuss over."

"She never married?"

"She's too independent and headstrong to put up with a husband."

"Like her niece?"

Her chin came up and she gave him a cold stare. "That's none of your business."

Nicholas smiled and hummed to himself, not put off by her caustic retort. He stole a quick glance out of the corner of his eye to find her head averted. A week was a long time; a very long time to be together where they would be forced to get along with each other.

He steered the Jeep along a stretch of a seemingly deserted back road and pulled into the parking lot behind a restaurant. "I've stopped so we can get something to eat," he informed her. "I doubt if we'll eat again before we get to where we're going late tonight."

Dyana unbuckled her seat belt, trying to ease the soreness in her knee. Sitting with her leg in the same position caused it to stiffen. "You're going to have to help me down," she said, hating the feeling of helplessness.

Nicholas opened the door on her side and reached out to help her out of the automobile. He held her suspended in the air effortlessly, then set her on her feet. Her eyes were level with his for a moment and she could see the dark centers in their depths. She was so close she was able to detect a light film of moisture on his upper lip and a small half-moon scar high on his left cheekbone.

"Lean against the bumper and I'll massage your leg."

Her hands went to his shoulders as he hunkered down to raise the hem of her dress to massage her bare leg and knee. Relaxing, she gave in to his searching fingers, marveling that his touch and presence gave her a sense of safeness. How would it be, she thought, to belong to Nicholas Bradshaw? To belong to him totally? "Where are we going in New Hampshire?" she sighed, enjoying his healing hands.

Nicholas stood, dropping an arm around her shoulders.

"Bristol. It's a tiny town where a friend of mine runs an exquisite country inn. It will afford us the privacy we need to work on the manuscript without visitors or telephones. I only left her telephone number with your aunt, Michael and Paul with strict instructions that they contact us only if it is a matter of life or death." The fingers of his left hand caught in her hair. "Now, how about an early dinner, Miss Randolph?"

She suffered his closeness, leaning against him to support her aching limb. The restaurant overlooked the Hudson River. "Where are we?" she asked looking around.

"Yonkers. This place is called The Lighthouse. The view, the food and the service is excellent."

He was right. The warm weather allowed for outdoor dining and they sat on the restaurant's patio enjoying the cooling breezes coming off the majestic Hudson and the verdant lushness of the Jersey coast on the opposite bank. Large and small sailing vessels floated fluidly on the calm surface of the river, the passengers waving as they sailed past.

Nicholas squinted against the bright sunlight. "Maybe one night we'll come back for a late dinner. The backdrop of the darkened sky and the sparkling stars always makes for a romantic setting."

Dyana lowered the chilled glass of Perrier and stared at the stunningly virile man staring at her. "Do you usually combine business with romance, Nicholas?"

"Never. But somehow with you I find myself doing a lot of things I normally do *not* do."

Her stomach muscles tightened. "Why am I the exception?" Why did she always find herself questioning him?

He leaned forward, resting his chin on his hand. His brow furrowed. "I don't know what it is about you but you upset my equilibrium. I've been a lot of places and I've known more than my share of women and none of them have ever affected me the way you have." His frown disappeared as he raised his eyebrows. "You're different, unique, and that alone makes you special." He took a sip of his wine, his eyes never leaving her face. "Lovely Dyana, Roman goddess of the moon and the hunt," he whispered in his deep voice. "Perhaps knowing I'll have to chase you will make it all the more exciting."

"What makes you think I'll allow you to catch me?" she asked. "What makes you think I need you or if I'd even want you?" she said, asking still another question.

"You're so full of questions and so unwilling to answer the ones I'd like to put to you. That's because you're afraid. Afraid of giving what you're capable of offering a man." He held up a hand when she opened her mouth to refute his statement. "And before you ask me what, I'll tell you."

"The worldly Nicholas Bradshaw has all of the answers," she snapped angrily.

He smiled. "Not all of them, but I know you're capable of giving a man your love and everything else he'd need in a relationship. Michael has been a lucky recipient."

"That's where you're so wrong. We share nothing but friendship."

His smile vanished quickly. "I do believe you're contradicting yourself, Dyana. You've hosted his parties and acted as his date at many a social event during the past few years. I caught a glimpse of you last year when you were draped all over his body at a publishing award event."

Her eyes flashed fire. "Looks are deceiving."

"I can remember everything about you that night," he continued as if she hadn't spoken. "Your hair was swept to one side and you wore a red silk rose behind your right ear. Your dress was a red and black strapless little thing . . ."

"Stop it!"

He stared at the tortured expression on her face. A spasm of pain gnawed at her innards when she thought of how the gossip had sometimes upset Michael whenever he overheard someone remark about his relationship with her. Had she really been that selfish when she told him to ignore the lewd, disparaging comments about their ages and enjoy their friendship?

She lowered her chin and stared at the salad on the plate

in front of her. "Michael and I are only friends, Nicholas. Can you believe that?"

He reached out to hold her chin firmly and raised her head until her eyes were level with his. "I believe you, Dyana." Tenderness turned his eyes to a soft, dark gray. "I'm sorry. Let's not begin our time together by fighting."

She gave him a bright smile and turned her attention to the sumptuous meal on the table. They ended with generous slices of cheesecake and coffee.

"I have a little place north of Tarrytown," he said when she saw signs indicating the Tappan Zee Bridge.

His little place turned out to be a complex of several buildings on a large estate. The main house was a superb Elizabethan manor house situated on a high bluff overlooking the river. She restrained her surprise when entering a majestic high-ceiling living room with two stone fireplaces facing each other. The dining room, with a view of the Hudson, was flanked by a new gourmet kitchen and had access to a lovely terrace. Six bedrooms and seven baths were set aside for spacious and convenient family living with enough room for guests either in the main house or in a private refurbished two-bedroom cottage.

She tried memorizing where everything was, the library in particular with a fireplace and the walls filled from floor to ceiling with books. Nicholas also showed her a housekeeper's suite and a three-car garage. A newly resurfaced tennis court and an oversized heated pool contributed to the private country club ambience of the magnificently landscaped property. The timber, stone, stucco and slate home was the most beautiful structure she had ever seen.

"Come, Dyana. Let me show you my favorite part of the property before we leave." He led her to a converted carriage house which housed interconnecting studios. White plank walls and dark wood beams crisscrossing the ceilings had transformed a former hayloft into a functional living area.

A desk in front of a wall of glass facing east allowed for

unlimited light during the daylight hours. To the right of the desk was a word processor, several typewriters and a tape recorder. Here, as in the library, the floor-to-ceiling shelves were packed tightly with books. Tucked away in a corner was a platform bed covered with a chintz comforter in a floral pattern of gray and mauve while large pillows in solid mauve, gray and white were tossed on the king-size bed. The cozy alcove also held a television, radio and video recorder.

He caught her fingers, squeezing them gently. "I work here most of the time. There's something about this room that allows you to get caught up in your work and forget there's a world outside."

She glanced at the thick white rug on the bleached flooring and the sunlight pouring in through the wall of glass and understood. This studio, suspended high above the water, allowed for a sense of weightlessness where the sky, forested woods and the solitude fused with the beauty of nature and creative energy to produce the powerfully written works Nicholas Bradshaw was known for.

"The next room should be a little more of interest to you," he murmured mysteriously as he led her into still another studio. He flipped a switch and the room was flooded with light from overhanging track lights.

Her mouth gaped in awe at the contents of the large studio. Every inch of wall space was covered with photographs. Stepping into the room, she noted each photo had been labeled and dated. Her eyes caught and she was mesmerized by the faces of black men, women and children staring at her, their faces echoing happiness, disappointment, fear and hope. She read the caption, "Mississippi Sharecroppers in the Promised Land." It was a photograph of a family who had arrived in Harlem amidst a stack of steamer trunks and cardboard suitcases held together with lengths of rope and belts. From the reticent expressions on the faces of the family of seven, Dyana wondered if the farmer perhaps regretted transporting his family to a strange city, teeming with millions of people all eager to exist in a crowded place of noise and bricks.

Another showed a winter scene of a group of unemployed men huddled around a large tin drum from which a fire blazed brightly for warmth. She spied another of a trio of young black girls jumping double Dutch on Eighth Avenue beneath the elevated track of the subway. Other children played under the watchful eyes of adults leaning out of the windows of tenement buildings rising above the clamor of the street traffic from streetcars and horse-drawn pushcarts and the crush of elegantly attired people below.

She found herself transfixed by row after row of prints that told of an era long past and of the hearty souls who once lived, loved and bred to keep a very unique neighborhood viable. "Where did you get these?" she asked, her eyes bright with excitement and respect.

"I bought them from a woman who was my landlady when I went to Columbia," he replied close to her ear when he stood next to her. "When she discovered my obsession for photography she pulled out these old faded prints. Years later I purchased them from her, restored them and gave her a copy of each as a gift."

"I suppose you took all of the others?" She waved her hand around the room.

He nodded. "The ones on that wall were from when I toured all of the states. These nearest you are from my overseas travel. The only ones not displayed are the scenes of the war." He had no desire to relive his year in Vietnam.

She shook her head in disbelief. There had to be more than two thousand framed, labeled and dated prints on the walls. "Where do you do your developing?"

He led her into a small room which served as his darkroom. "There's a special cooling system to keep the temperature regulated to sustain the quality of the film and developing chemicals," he explained.

Dyana felt as if her head was spinning when he closed the door and flicked on an overhead light. The room appeared so much smaller when his large body pressed close to hers, not permitting her the space she needed to breathe comfortably. He flicked off the light and opened the door. "One more room and we'll have finished the tour, Miss Randolph. This one I'll bet will be your favorite."

He was correct. This room was not as large as the others but it transfixed her as no other. She was astounded by the priceless art pieces nestled casually on walls, tables and the floor. A massive African tribal mask and spear, framed Far East prints of calligraphy, works by Matisse, Degas, Miró, Chagall and the cubist-surrealist forms of Picasso were all vying for attention on a wall behind an antique drop-leaf table. The English table of pine was covered with sketches and the sculpture of Frederic Remington, fragments of Indian pottery and the fragile remains of a Navaho rug.

"I know nothing about art, Dyana," he said quickly before she could ask about his phenomenal collection. An expression of innocence softened his features. "I've allowed someone to talk me into buying these things for investment purposes. I don't know a Picasso from a van Gogh," he confessed. "Lenses, languages and a typewriter are my speed. I'm totally ignorant where it concerns music or art."

She gazed lovingly at the Remington sculpture. "Your representative has excellent taste in art," she stated candidly. "Would you mind disclosing your source?"

"Not at all. Her name is Marva Jackson."

Dyana reacted visibly when she heard the name. She had read several years before that Nicholas Bradshaw and Marva Jackson were romantically linked to one another. Marva had become an authority on primitive art while studying in West Africa and made a name for herself when she returned to Europe with an exceptional collection of primitive art forms.

"Is she still living in London?"

"She keeps a flat in London, but prefers the south of France."

His voice reflected respect and something more. Dyana wondered if he still thought about her or was in love with her.

"I remember when her show came to Philadelphia. My high school art history class went to the museum and the boys were astonished by the accoutrements of tribal warfare. One boy everyone called Butch waited until the museum guard's back was turned to grab a spear and hurl it across the room like a javelin."

A deep unrestrained laugh erupted from Nicholas's throat. "Let's get ready to leave. We have quite a few miles to cover today. And I'd also like to hear about this column of yours Michael has told me so much about."

FOUR

Dyana walked the length of the circular driveway, waiting for Nicholas to change. A large bag by the door indicated he hadn't altered the habit he'd acquired when he was on foreign assignment; he was always ready to leave the moment he received a call.

A large black and white cat ambled toward her, brushing against her bare legs. She leaned down to stroke the silky fur. "How are you?" The cat meowed softly. "What's your name, pretty girl?"

"Her name is Buttons. It was the only thing I could think of when I saw the white face with the tiny black nose." Buttons flopped down on Nicholas's sneaker-covered feet.

She straightened, her breath catching in her chest. How different he looked in a pair of tight faded jeans and an equally faded gray short-sleeve sweatshirt. Her gaze swept from his broad chest to the cat wiggling on her master's foot. The feline's claws were fastened in the laces and Nicholas smiled when her paws became entangled in their length.

"Not today, Buttons." He knelt to extract the cat. "Go annoy Mrs. Peterson. Better yet, be nice to her. She's going to be feeding you for the next week."

"She's very affectionate for a cat."

"She's somewhat neurotic. At times she believes she's a dog. Believe it or not I play fetch with her."

Dyana laughed. "I wonder how she would get along with George?"

Nicholas picked up his bag, his free hand going to her elbow. "With George's appetite, he'd probably have Buttons for dinner."

"Tell me about your proposed column."

"I plan for it to be sort of a potpourri," she began excitedly as Nicholas began the long drive which would end in Bristol, New Hampshire. "A little bit of art with a dash of music and drama and a pinch of North American folklore."

He threw back his head, laughing. "It sounds like an artistic stew."

"That's exactly what I plan for *Regions* to be. Many cities and regions of the country have been undergoing a renaissance and I want my column to reflect the changes in these areas, hopefully igniting a similar cultural revival in others."

He raised his eyebrows, not taking his eyes off the road. "Do you really think it'll spark our readers' interest?"

"Yes. Music is not only rock and roll, but jazz, classical, gospel, country-western, Casals, Ellington and Dixieland. The same can be said for art and folk festivals and historic landmark districts. What I want to do is stress their uniqueness and the impact on the differing regions of North America."

"Do you honestly think that you know enough about all of these subjects to be able to cover them intelligently month after month?"

"No," she admitted. "But qualified contributing writers should."

His mouth tightened. "I don't doubt your writing ability, Dyana, and I'm aware of your knowledge of music, but what I question is the coverage of the theater and folk festivals. Would it mean your traveling to different cities to cover the events and openings?"

Her back stiffened when she registered his reluctance. "If it can be arranged, I'd like to cover one or two a year."

His expression was unreadable when he hesitated. "Let me think about it, Dyana. After all I do have an editorial board to answer to. It will have to be a group decision."

She drew in a deep breath, knowing the possibility of her attaining her own column was still possible, and picked at the soft fabric of her dress to spread it out over her knees in a smoothing motion.

Nicholas had decided to play by the rules when deciding on her column. He was going to present it for approval, even though he being who he was was enough to give her an answer now. Paul Scranton had allowed him absolute autonomy as long as it benefited *Pinnacle*. If he had gotten Paul to agree to Carl Murphy's advance, why not her column?

The increasing rush hour traffic slowed their progress when they entered the city limits of Hartford. Insurance companies and high-tech corporate headquarters, housed in stately old structures along with glass and steel, rose majestically in the capital city's skyline as the glow of headlights glimmered eerily in the gunmetal gray of the afternoon. The darkening sky, rising humidity and wind indicated impending rain.

"It looks as if it's going to come down at any moment," she remarked, then jumped when a flash of lightning followed by a thundering roll of thunder shook the heavens. A limp, crumpled tissue failed to blot the dampness on her cheeks. Nicholas had turned off the air conditioning and rolled down the windows when traffic had slowed to where they seemed to inch along at a rate of only five miles an hour. The heat and humidity became oppressive. Everything was sticking to her moist flesh.

"How about if I try to get off at the next exit?" There was another roll of thunder and her response was lost. Nicholas took a quick glance over his right shoulder and flipped the directional signal. Lightning lit up the interior of the Jeep and his eyes were luminous when they searched her face. "Are you all right?"

She gave him a weak smile, nodding. "I'm fine." She wasn't about to admit to him that thunderstorms unnerved her.

Miraculously, Nicholas was able to change lanes as he maneuvered and pulled off the turnpike at the next exit. He switched on the radio and the announcer's voice was barely audible above the crack of lightning and the violent explosion of thunder. Dyana closed her eyes and pressed back against the seat when she heard the warning of severe thunderstorms and a tornado watch for the tri-state region.

Wet fat drops splattered the windshield and soon the fastest speed of the wipers were no match for the raging torrent. The inside of the four-wheeler became a suffocating tomb until the air conditioning lowered the temperature. Massive branches of large trees writhed in the wind, resembling a macabre ballet.

"Look for a motel or hotel, Dyana," Nicholas ordered, squinting through the sheet of water sliding down the windshield. "I can't see more than a foot in front of the lights."

It was another half hour before she spotted a neon sign indicating clean, comfortable, private bungalows. "Over here," she shouted. "To your right."

She cowered in the corner of the Jeep waiting for Nicholas to return. Outside of the vehicle, nature seemed out of control with its fury. The moaning sounds of the wind, lightning and thunder increased her uneasiness. What was taking him so long to register?

The door swung open and the driving rain soaked her already moist flesh. "We're in luck. We've managed to get the last one," Nicholas informed her as he slipped behind the wheel. The short distance from the manager's office to the Jeep had left him soaked. He turned the key in the ignition. "There are several conventions and shows going on in town and apparently beds are at a premium," he said.

Safe haven. That was what the bungalow had become. Light from table lamps added a warm golden glow to the wood-paneled walls and polished pine floors. Comfortable furniture, covered with fabric in earth tones, was scattered throughout the large living-dining room. A stack of wood stood against the wall near a fireplace.

Rivulets of water dripped from her hair down her back and into her face and she shivered when the coolness touched her warm skin. Dyana slipped out of her shoes and placed them by the fireplace. Turning, she noticed a flight of winding stairs leading to a loft. She knew without walking up those stairs that it led to a bedroom. The setting was perfect for a honeymoon.

The door opened and Nicholas entered, carrying their bags. He dropped them to the floor and leaned against the closed door. His face, hidden in the shadows, was unreadable. "You can use the upstairs bath to change and I'll take the one down here," he suggested softly.

Dyana headed for the stairs, leaving him to follow with her single piece of luggage. Her tender knee threatened to give way, but she managed to make it to the spacious loft without his assistance. The quiet whisper of her breathing and soft patter of her bare feet along with the squeak of the rubber soles of Nicholas's shoes were the only sounds in the space. It was as if the storm had ceased to exist.

Nicholas put her bag down beside an enormous brass bed. She jumped when his hand touched her damp shoulder, turning her around to face him. The rain had plastered his short hair to his scalp and the heat from his large body seeped into her chilled one. She was paralyzed, unable to move. Again she fell under his spell. Not once had he demonstrated that he was interested in her other than she had intrigued him because she appeared different and mysterious; intrigued him because of her relationship with Michael.

"Get out of those wet clothes, Dyana," he said in the now familiar soft and soothing tone.

His hand dropped and she felt distant, alone. "You do the same," she returned. "I don't need you sick where you won't be able to drive. I don't trust my knee to manipulate both clutch and gas pedals, Mr. Bradshaw."

He smiled broadly. "Yes ma'am."

She hummed a popular love ballad as she stepped into the tub under a warm flow of water. She shampooed and conditioned her hair, reveling in the relaxed feeling which refused to vanish. As much as she tried, she couldn't shake the feeling of safeness and protection which surrounded her. Nicholas appeared to be everything Steven hadn't been, and although she had thought herself in love with her ex-fiancé she still hadn't felt comfortable with him. There always was that tiny piece of security which eluded her. She hadn't realized what it was until it was too late.

A blow dryer with a large comb attachment left her relaxed hair straight and shining. She curled her bangs with a curling iron but left the back uncurled when she swept the blunt-cut ends up into a ponytail and secured it with an elastic band. The warm shower had been a balm to her stiff knee and she flexed it in a pair of melon cotton slacks. A matching camp shirt and navy espadrilles proved to be equally comfortable.

She walked out of the bathroom, stopping when she saw Nicholas, bare-chested on the large bed. Long, arched feet were visible from where she stood staring at the prone figure. Even though the muted light cast shadows over his body, she still was able to discern his features relaxed in sleep. She moved closer, unable to pull her gaze away from the expanse of bare flesh covered with a mat of thick black curling hair that tapered down to a thin line to disappear into the waistband of his jeans. These jeans were newer than the ones he'd worn earlier; repeated washings hadn't given them the pale blue-gray shade of the others. One large muscular arm was thrown over his head and she was transfixed as she stood motionless staring at the man who made her forget her reason for shutting out the existence of younger men. What a fool; Nicholas's ex-wife had been a fool for leaving him. He was perfect, too perfect.

She moved closer, silently and methodically. Everything about Nicholas Bradshaw screamed brilliance, security and unabashed masculinity: his gentle touch, the soft sound of his voice and his penetrating gaze. She drew her lower lip between her teeth. Why couldn't she have fallen in love with Nicholas instead of Steven? Why couldn't he be the man she'd given her heart and pledged her future to?

Turning away, she made her way down the stairs to the living room. She pushed back the floor-to-ceiling drapes. The storm continued its assault, soaking and lashing the city with its unleashed fury and she wondered how long they would be forced to remain in Connecticut and possibly have to share the one bed.

Dyana cradled her head on a soft, fluffy throw pillow on the love seat and midway between late afternoon and nightfall she slept, shutting out the storm and Nicholas. It was nearly eight o'clock when she awoke to near total darkness except for a flickering glow from the fireplace. Disoriented, she glanced around at her strange surroundings and tried easing the pain in her stiffened leg with her fingers.

"There's been a power failure," came Nicholas's voice somewhere in the blackness of the large space.

"What time is it?" she asked in a husky voice.

"Seven-fifty."

She stretched, reminding him of a cat. "How long has it been out?"

Nicholas stood, moving into the glow of the flame. "About an hour." He made his way across the room to where she lay on the love seat. "Everything's down: electricity and telephones." He sat down, enveloping her with the scent of his haunting cologne.

She swung her feet to the floor. "It sounds as if the rain has stopped."

"It stopped a little while ago, but fallen power lines are the problem." His hand went to her knee, massaging it. "How's your leg holding up?"

She closed her eyes against the soothing motion. "It only stiffens when I don't use it," she murmured.

"I'm sorry," came his hoarse whisper in the semidarkness of the room.

"Sorry for what?" she replied.

"Sorry for hurting you."

She reopened her eyes, searching for his troubled expression in the shadows. "No more, Nicholas!" she shouted. "I thought we'd settled that issue."

His hand stopped its ministration. "It's not easy when I see you grimace and limp when you don't think I'm aware of it. Heroic Miss Dyana Randolph wanting to appear invincible. There's nothing wrong with hurting."

"I hurt, Nicholas. I hurt just like everyone else."

"Sure you do, Dee," he said, using her family's nickname. His hands moved to her shoulders pulling her close until his face was only inches away. "But you've managed to hide the hurt very well." One hand curved around her neck until her cheek lay on a hard shoulder. "When are you going to stop hiding?" he whispered against her ear.

Dyana gave in to his strength, the clean smell of his laundered shirt and the coaxing sound of his voice when she melted against his chest. Could she afford to tell this man, a stranger, of her past? Would he condemn her as a silly girl masquerading as a woman who had allowed herself to become involved with her instructor?

"What is it you want to know?" she asked in a trembling voice.

"Everything," he replied, tightening his embrace.

"Steven Chapman was my music instructor," she began, "and he showed me the beauty of the world as I had never envisioned it before. Initially, I took one of his classes, then all of them. It began with having coffee together after field trips and escalated to intimate dinners at his apartment. What had begun so innocently as a student-instructor relationship quickly turned into a relationship which transcended the bounds of common sense and reality. I told myself that I was in love with him and unconsciously surrendered my future to a man who had assumed control of my life."

She pulled away, feeling the need to put some space between them. Clasping her fingers together, she laid them in her lap. She swallowed, trying to formulate the words she had never uttered to another living soul. The crackling of burning wood sounded like an exploding bomb in the stillness. Nicholas made no attempt to touch her and his presence said more than words of encouragement.

"I was willing to marry him knowing he couldn't be a faithful husband. My obsession with him obscured all of his shortcomings. I entered a work-study program and with his intervention I was placed at the conservatory where he was an associate director. I was required to work fifteen hours each week but sometimes I put in more than twice that amount just to be able to be with him. In my naïveté I failed to notice his lack of affection and rationalized the pressures of his position and teaching schedule for the changes in his personality."

She couldn't go on. Memories of Steven's infidelity choked her. She lost touch with the present until she felt Nicholas's hand prying her fingers from the front of his shirt. His thumb touched her cold mouth before his head lowered to breathe a breath of warmth on her lips. "Dyana," he whispered gently, then settled his mouth over hers and coaxed her into responding.

Dyana felt the healing touch of his questing mouth and pressed closer, losing herself in the kiss and savoring his protection. She pulled back and buried her face in his throat. Her breath was coming quickly. "Steven gave me a key to his apartment when we became engaged and told me never to use it unless it was an emergency. I arrived at the conservatory on Monday to find him out sick. I became alarmed only because when I'd left him the prior evening he hadn't shown any signs or mentioned that he wasn't feeling well. I telephoned his apartment and when I didn't get a response, I decided to stop by after work.

"I found my fiancé with another girl from one of our classes together. I don't know who was more surprised, Steven, Anne or me. He was quick to soothe my anger, saying there was nothing going on and that he loved me too much to risk our future by fooling around with another woman."

He went rigid. "You believed him?"

"I believed him," she admitted, ashamed of her gullibility. "I paid for believing him when he didn't show up at the church the day of our wedding." Fingers of steel tightened painfully on her arms. "He sent me a letter a week later asking that I forgive him. He claimed he loved me but that he was afraid to commit himself to one woman. He had accepted a position as director of music for a high school in

St. Louis. It appears that neither of us could remain in Philadelphia. For me the memories were too painful."

Nicholas cupped her head between his hands, his eyes racing quickly over her face. "He lied to you. He didn't love you Dyana. If he did, he would've never left you."

The room was flooded with light and both of them blinked against the unaccustomed brightness. The power had been restored. Nicholas seemed reluctant to release her and she didn't want him to. She wanted him to hold her—for a long time.

She was the first to pull away. "I'd better get my things together," she suggested. She heard him curse under his breath, hearing only part of it when he "damned the lights."

"I'll carry your bag," he called up to her when she made her way up the stairs to the loft.

She retrieved her dress and underwear from the rod over the tub and folded them neatly. Nicholas picked up her bag and glanced at the rumpled quilt on the bed where he'd slept, before turning his fiery green gaze on her. There was a bold, open invitation in their depths, and she wondered if he regretted having to leave. She let out a sigh, not realizing she'd been holding her breath. What would've happened if the power hadn't been restored at that moment?

"Let's get ready, Nicholas. We have quite a few miles to cover tonight," she said, repeating what he'd said only hours before.

Dyana had seen so many small towns and towering pine trees and mountains that they all began to look the same. She was unable to distinguish Massachusetts from Vermont or New Hampshire except by road markers. It was midnight when they crossed the border from Vermont into New Hampshire and Nicholas stopped at a rest area along the interstate to stretch his legs. The Green Mountains loomed in the distance like uneven humps on massive buffaloes.

He helped her down from the Jeep and she breathed in deeply, filling her lungs with dry pine-filled air, staring up at the star-littered sky. "Lovely, pastoral New England."

"It is lovely, isn't it?" he agreed, placing a cotton sweater around her shoulders, tying the sleeves around her neck. "I don't want you getting a chill," he explained when she looked up at him.

She snuggled against the warm material, retying the sleeves and inhaling the cologne clinging to the garment. She couldn't pull her eyes away from his face. It was as if he had begun to seep into her brain, her soul, to batter down her defenses until she was helpless to resist him.

"Do you want something to eat or drink?" he asked.

"No, thank you."

"I think I'll have a cup of coffee."

It was two in the morning when they arrived at Lucy's Victorian Inn advertising bed and breakfast in the town of Bristol and Nicholas laid his forehead against the steering wheel in a gesture which registered his weariness. "We're here," he sighed in relief.

She looked out at a large house, seeing very little of its charm in the darkness. Unbuckling her seat belt, she limped down, moaning when her entire body protested. A light went on in one of the upstairs rooms and it was only minutes later that a woman's voice shattered the silence.

"You must be getting old, Nicky. Years ago you would've made the drive in five hours instead of ten."

His arm curved around Dyana's waist, supporting her sagging body. "I was carrying precious cargo this time, Lucille. Show me to the most comfortable bed in the house and I'll love you forever." His free arm circled the shoulders of a petite figure clothed in a chenille robe.

Lucille patted his cheek, grinning. "I happen to have the most comfortable bed, and I don't think Dan would appreciate you sleeping with his wife, even if he's on the other side of the world." She stepped around Nicholas to smile at Dyana. "Is this the precious cargo you were referring to?" She extended a tiny hand. "Come inside where I can show you a little Yankee hospitality."

Dyana took the hand and Lucille led her into the house. She stepped into a foyer surrounded with Tiffany glass windows and dark mahogany woodwork. Glossy parquet floors, covered with colorful rag rugs, mirrored her reflection. Wood panels of lacquered and varnished beech, graceful curved cabinets in rare inlay wood captured her attention, and she gaped at the beauty of the interior of the Victorian structure.

"I'm Lucy Chandler." A friendly smile, dark brown hair and sparkling clear gray eyes went along with the voice.

Dyana returned the smile with a tired one of her own. "Dyana Randolph."

The gray eyes examined her quickly. "Nicky told me he was bringing a surprise, but I couldn't imagine what it was. You're quite an eyeful."

Dyana felt her face heat up. "Thank you."

"Can I get you anything before I show you your bedroom?"

Her body screamed from the long drive and she shook her head. "Thank you, no. All I want to see is a bathtub and bed."

Lucy led her through a drawing room and up a flight of stairs to the second floor. A warm light from a Tiffany lamp lit the area, highlighting closed doors to several rooms.

"This one will be yours. It has an adjoining bath you won't have to share with other guests."

Dyana was fatigued past the point where she'd care whether she would or would not have to share a bathroom with other guests or with Nicholas. She doubted whether she could remain awake long enough to wash her face.

She awoke to the sound of voices outside of the closed door to the bedroom and rolled over on her back to stare up at the crocheted canopy above the bed. Bright sunlight poured through lace panels at the windows. She groped for her watch on the bedside table and peered at the gold hands and dots on the tiny black face. It was after one; she had been asleep for almost twelve hours.

Swinging her legs over the side of the bed, she pulled the nightgown over her head and headed for the bathroom, aware of the lack of stiffness in her knee for the first time in days. She was able to shower and brush her teeth in record time. She slipped into a pair of jeans and a tee shirt and jogging shoes, then emptied her luggage, hanging skirts, blouses and slacks in a large walk-in closet.

Thirty minutes later she found herself in a spacious kitchen with Lucy Chandler whose arms were covered to the elbows with flour. Wisps of short curling dark brown hair clung to her moist forehead. Attractive dimples winked when she looked up and smiled.

"I suppose you're looking for your boyfriend?"

"Where's Nicholas?" she asked, ignoring the reference to her and Nicholas being romantically linked.

Lucy rinsed her arms and hands in a stainless steel sink. "He's been up for hours. After breakfast he locked himself in the room off the porch. Mentioned something about having a lot of work to do."

Dyana groaned. "He's been working while I was sleeping."

"That's because he's not as bright as you are. He looks as if a truck hit him. Are you ready to eat something?"

She wanted to refuse so she could begin work on the manuscript but couldn't. It had been twenty-four hours since her last meal. "Some coffee and a blueberry muffin will do just fine," she suggested when spotting a milk-glass platter filled with muffins.

"You look as if you need more than coffee and a muffin," Lucy said when she surveyed the slim figure in a pair of fitted jeans.

You're a fine one to talk, Dyana thought. Lucy was barely five feet and weighed about ninety-five pounds.

"How long have you known Nicholas?" Dyana asked after sitting down at a massive round oak table in the center of the kitchen.

"Nicky and I practically grew up together. My father was his father's aide when we lived in Europe."

"You were an Army brat?"

Lucy set a plate filled with several muffins on the table in front of her. "Don't remind me. We moved around so much I thought I was a gypsy. I guess that's the reason I won't travel more than twenty miles in any given month."

Dyana took a bite of a fluffy berry-filled muffin. "Living in a different country every couple of years sounds like fun." Her childhood traveling consisted of visiting her grandparents in Savannah every summer.

Lucy placed an enameled coffeepot on a burner. "I'm too much like my mother," she admitted. "She hated military life and complained bitterly until my father put in his twenty years and retired. Nicky's father still hasn't gotten his fill. Colonel Bradshaw has retired, yet he and his wife continue to travel." She put a jar of homemade strawberry preserves next to the muffins. "How long have you and Nicky been seeing each other?"

Dyana wiped her mouth with a cloth napkin, forcing back a smile. "You think Nicholas and I are involved with each other?"

Lucy shrugged her shoulders. "Why else? He's never brought another woman here in the past. I thought he requested separate rooms because both of you were too tired after the drive to do anything except sleep."

Dyana shook her head, chuckling. "Nicholas and I only *work* together. We're here to work on a project so we won't be disturbed."

Lucy gave her a wide-eyed look, blushing brightly. "I'm sorry. I didn't intend to assume . . ."

"There's nothing to be sorry about," she interrupted. "Nicholas is my boss and nothing more."

"Does that mean I can order you to get me a cup of coffee, Miss Randolph?"

She shifted in the chair, experiencing a light flutter in the pit of her stomach when she saw his tall figure in the doorway. His usual faded jeans hugged slim hips while a short-sleeve white cotton shirt was stretched over his broad chest and wide shoulders, blatantly emphasizing his well-conditioned body. Torn tan moccasins covered sockless feet as he leaned against the archway, one foot crossed over the other.

"You don't need any more coffee," said Lucy. "You need sleep."

"I'll take a nap later, Mother Lucy." He walked into the kitchen and flopped down wearily on a chair across from Dyana. He flashed a tired smile. "How are you feeling?"

"Wonderful," she admitted. "I was asleep before my head touched the pillow."

"I know," he said quietly. "I heard the snoring across the hall."

"I don't snore!"

"How would you know?" he teased.

She felt her cheeks burn. "I don't. But . . . but I'm certain I don't."

"Stop teasing her, Nicky," Lucy warned, knowing him well enough to know what he was inferring. The kitchen was filled with the fragrant aroma of freshly ground brewed coffee and she poured the steaming liquid into three large mugs. "Take your coffee and off to bed with you," she ordered Nicholas. "Whatever you're working on Dyana can pick up."

Dyana remembered the Murphy manuscript. "How does it read?"

His eyes became a sparkling gray. "Fascinating," he replied between sips of coffee. "You can begin to put what I've completed into the word processor."

Lucy raised her mug to her lips. "Can you tell me what it is you're working on?"

"It's top secret, Lucy," he said.

She lowered the cup slowly, frowning. "You're not using my inn for military activities, are you?"

Nicholas smiled. "Stop creating spy plots, Lucy."

She waved her hand. "I can deal with anything but the military. I turn off the television when anything resembling the military is shown, and that includes the commercials."

Nicholas winked at Dyana. "Don't let her fool you. She saw *Platoon* three times." Lucy reached for a terry towel and snapped it at his head, missing him when he ducked. "Good afternoon, ladies. I'm off to bed." He bowed from the waist and backed out of the kitchen.

Lucy exchanged an amused look with Dyana. "He's quite a character; that is if you get to know the real Nicholas Bradshaw and not the one his publicist has created for the masses. Not once could I ever believe all of the ridiculous things said or written about him. The only depiction that came close was when '60 Minutes' did a piece about the authenticity of *Platoon,* and Nicky was interviewed because his first book with the photographs was as real a picture as one could get of the war without actually being there."

Dyana thought about what she'd heard about Nicholas before meeting him. She, like most of the others, was aware of his reputation of running a magazine like a storm trooper, expecting his edicts to be followed without question and demanding complete loyalty. She'd spent less than three hours at *Pinnacle* with Nicholas assuming full responsibility while Michael functioned as a figurehead, and the change was apparent. She wondered how much of his father's military training had been transferred to the son.

"I'd better get to work," she informed Lucy. "I don't want to be court-martialed for not following orders."

"I wouldn't worry too much, Dyana. Even if you decided to goldbrick for the next year, Nicky would forgive you. Come, let me show you where you'll be working."

Lucy led her to a large room which ran half the length of the front porch and along one side of the house. As with the other rooms in the Victorian mansion, this space was filled with exquisite antiques and furnishings. Turkey-red lacquer walls were complemented by draperies of off-white sailcloth. Overstuffed chairs in red and sand beige and a cotton rag area rug in red, pink and brown tones covered a pale carpet.

Four acres of woods bordered the property and the trees along this side of the house had been cleared to let in the natural outdoor light. She peered out of the window to see pine-covered mountain peaks in the distance. The gentle sound of chirping birds and a light breeze rustling leaves became nature's melodious symphony. There was a soft thud and she turned to see a large black and white cat staring at her. Its color and markings reminded her of Buttons as it stood motionless, the golden eyes following her as she gestured for it to come to her. It backed up toward the door and meowed softly, indicating it wanted to escape. Dyana crossed the room to open the door and the cat scooted past her in a flash of black and white.

She picked up the manuscript from a walnut double-bonnet secretary and began reading Nicholas's legible print along the margins. He'd been right when he said Carl Murphy was not a writer; her first attempt at writing was superior to what Murphy had put down on his opening page.

The accounting was nonfictional although it read like a work of fiction. Carl Murphy had related facts she thought only appeared in films and she wondered if the Justice Department, if made aware of the manuscript, would seek to suppress it. She uncovered the keyboard and switched on the monitor to the word processor. Inserting a disk, she punched in a code; the program was the same she'd used at the magazine.

She lost track of time as the sun sank below the horizon and an occasional guest arrived to stay at the inn. Her only visitor was the large cat who squeezed through the opening in the door to investigate the stranger invading its territory. Her fingers paused on the keys—this section wasn't going as smoothly as the others. Nicholas had rewritten a scene where Carl established his initial contact with a female operative. She typed a sentence, then deleted it. She reread what Nicholas had written. It wasn't working; somehow he had failed to develop the depth of this character as she related to Carl. She was flat and one dimensional.

She stored what she'd typed and stood up to stretch her cramped limbs. The storing completed, she backed up a copy of her work and slipped both disks into sleeves and placed them in a plastic box. It had taken her six hours to complete over fifty pages of typed manuscript; however, it hadn't taken more than several seconds to ascertain that Nicholas hadn't bothered with punctuating and had left that task for her.

"What are you doing here?" she asked, surprised when she saw Nicholas sitting on a window seat in her bedroom.

He rose to his feet, appearing refreshed. The shadows under his eyes were gone and he'd shaved, leaving his cheeks smooth and free of the stubble of an emerging beard. "Waiting for you. I was going to give you another fifteen minutes before coming down."

She turned the switch on the lamp, flooding the room with more light. "That would've been unnecessary. I finished all of your editing." She stared down at the lace doily on the bedside table, visually tracing the design. "But there's one section I don't feel comfortable with."

"The one where he meets Kira?"

She turned to meet his glowing eyes. "How did you know?"

"Didn't you check the wastebasket? I rewrote that scene at least eight times before settling on that version."

"She's too stiff, Nicholas. No one would ever believe she could seduce a man to get him to pass secrets for her."

Nicholas closed the space between them, giving her an intense look. "Will you rewrite Kira's scenes for me?"

Dyana sank down slowly to the bed, her eyes widening in shock. "I can't do that, Nicholas."

He dropped down beside her, holding her hands firmly within his. "You have to Dyana. You have to do it because I can't feel her; she's too complex. I've tried to get inside of her head and I've failed. She has to be able to think, to feel and to breathe real life!" He tightened his grip. "You can do it!"

His compelling eyes wouldn't allow her to draw a normal breath. His nearness projected an intoxicating vacuum of power. She didn't know how, but she was feeling what he was feeling and it was raw excitement spinning out of control. Their eyes locked, suspending them in a moment where they and their emotions became one.

"I'll try," she whispered, shuddering and collapsing against his chest. His heart pounded wildly under her ear and she knew she'd done the right thing.

"Thank you for being here when I need you. Thank you, darling," he sighed, burying his face in her hair and inhaling her delicate feminine fragrance.

The unconscious endearment haunted her long after Nicholas left. They were going out for dinner and she still was only half dressed. There had been another time when he'd called her darling and it was the only thing which had kept her from panicking.

Staring at her reflection in the mirror, she began to remove the heated rollers from her hair. Did he call all women darling or could she believe that he'd reserved it for the special ones, and dare she hope to believe that she was special? But he'd said she was special. Special for what purpose? Did he want to play with her, then toss her away when he tired of her or when she began to bore him?

Don't worry about a thing, girlfriend. Livvy's motto made her smile. Worry? Not Dyana Randolph. If Steven Chapman was trouble, Nicholas Bradshaw would be certain disaster. Somehow she wasn't equipped for the big leagues; and Nicholas was big league and prime time.

She slipped into a pale pink linen blouse, a pair of linen slacks and a lightweight jacket in a darker pink and bone-colored pumps with a low heel. Tonight she brushed her curling hair off her face and settled for a light coat of mascara on her lashes and a rosy shade of color for her mouth.

His eyes sparkled in appreciation when she walked into the living room, mirroring his reaction to her appearance.

FIVE

Dyana sat Indian-style on the grass watching Nicholas as he read what she'd written. She shifted uneasily, then stretched her legs out to take the pressure off her knee. She tried analyzing his reaction and failed. He'd supported his back against the trunk of a tree, pulling his knees up to where he rested the pad in his lap. She noted the length of his lashes on his cheekbones and the steady rising and falling of his chest; the slight lifting of an eyebrow behind a pair of black metal-rimmed glasses revealed nothing. Did he like her characterization of the female intelligence agent?

Not able to withstand the tension she stood up and walked a short distance from where they'd spent the past two hours writing and picnicking. Nicholas had decided not to edit any more of the manuscript until she'd developed the character Carl called Kira.

She'd read enough of the manuscript to discover that Kira was not beautiful but was what Carl had described as plain and lonely. Her aura of loneliness was what drew him to her and put his own life in jeopardy. And not once had he intimated that he'd engaged in a relationship which included a physical entanglement.

She walked along the grassy knoll following the flight of a snow-white butterfly. In two days she'd forgotten the noise and crowded streets of Manhattan to find a peace where she forgot to look at her watch to tell the time of day. It was as if she'd become locked in a time warp and didn't want to return to the hustling, bustling world of the urban jungle. She went to bed thinking of Nicholas and woke looking for him.

They worked well together. He usually rose early to write

so that she would have something to put into the computer, and when they dined together he refused to talk shop.

"Dyana!"

His wide grin was her answer. He liked what she'd written. She retraced her steps, running into his outstretched arms. Her arms went around his neck when he swung her high in the air. She squealed like an excited child as the sky, sun and leaves spun dizzily upon her upturned face. "Stop, Nicky! Please," she pleaded.

Nicholas tumbled to the grass, pulling her down with him and cushioning her body. His extraordinary eyes blazed with fire and some other unrecognizable emotion.

"You like it?" She couldn't stop the tremor in her voice.

Nicholas blinked slowly behind his glasses and reached up to remove them. He cradled her face between the palms of his large hands. His mood had changed so quickly it frightened her. There was no smile or glint of humor in his eyes. He was looking at her as if he were seeing her for the first time as his fingers inched through the curling hair falling to her shoulders. Her breath caught in her chest when he lowered his head to press a light kiss to her forehead. It was over as quickly as it had begun when he sprang to his feet, pulling her up with him.

"You've created an incredible character. Kira becomes a heroine instead of a femme fatale. You've made her so believable that anyone who reads the book can believe how Carl was taken in by her vulnerability." He threw his head back, grinning. "I can't believe it," he rasped, clenching both fists tightly. "You're wonderful, Dyana!"

His exuberance was contagious and she raised her face to the sky and whispered a small prayer of thanks. She was thankful she'd been given the opportunity to prove herself.

Nicholas startled her when his arms encircled her waist to pull her back against his chest. Her hands covered his and she relaxed in his embrace. His warm breath stirred the hair at her temple. "Let's pop the cork on that bottle of wine I saw Lucy sneak into the basket and celebrate," she suggested, raising her chin to glance up at his smiling face.

"I think we should take the rest of the afternoon off and celebrate. What do you think, Miss Randolph?"

Shrugging her shoulders, she cocked her head at an angle. "You're the boss, Mr. Bradshaw."

He picked her up again and swung her around. "I say it's party time!"

They became children once again as he continued to spin around while she pleaded with him to stop. The puffs of clouds blended in with the blueness of the sky as everything merged above her.

"I give up, Nicholas!" she cried over and over. She was breathless and slightly faint when he tumbled to the grass. She felt the dampness of his flesh through the cotton shirt. His breathing was normal while her heart pounded uncontrollably. Her arm lay over his flat stomach and inched up until her fingers were spread out over his chest.

He shifted until her head lay on his shoulder, and pushed back the hair sticking to her cheek. Sighing, she closed her eyes, a satisfied smile inching her lips upward.

"What are you smiling about?"

"I was wondering what would Paul and the other employees think if they saw us now."

His fingers traced the shape of her ear, her jaw and finally the outline of her mouth. "Why not give them something to talk about?" he said softly before leaning over to taste her mouth.

His kiss was gentle as a whisper and she thought she'd imagined it. Tears welled up behind her lids at his tenderness and she drank in his healing passion. Her hand moved up his solid chest to rest against his cheek.

Nicholas pulled back, his breath now coming quickly and she was trembling and there was nothing she could do to control it. Her lids came down to hide what she was unable to conceal in her golden brown eyes. Nicholas Bradshaw could not come to be more than her boss. There was no way she would allow that to happen.

"I think drinking wine is a safer way of celebrating, don't you think?"

"It may be safer but less fun," Nicholas teased, rolling over and coming to his feet. He held out his hand to her. "Come. Let's not waste the wine or the afternoon."

She raised the glass filled with a dark red burgundy, recognizing a return of the teasing twinkle in his eyes. "To Kira," she said, offering a toast.

He touched his glass to hers. "And Carl."

She started to bring the glass to her lips, then hesitated. "And *Pinnacle.*"

Nicholas nodded, his expression changing like quicksilver. Inhaling deeply, he stared at her, his glass suspended motionless. He clenched and unclenched his jaw, a muscle throbbing noticeably. Dyana held her breath as her pulses skipped erratically along her flesh.

"To us," he finally said and her hand shook when she brought the glass up to her lips.

The wine cooled, then warmed her throat and chest. She looked away to stare at several ants making their way along a discarded piece of bread crust. "To us," she repeated.

Nicholas rested an elbow on a raised knee, the half-filled glass dangling from long brown fingers. "Did I embarrass you, Dyana?"

Her head came up quickly. "No."

He drained the glass with one swallow, setting it on the grass. "Good." Sinking back onto the grass, he folded his arms under his head. "Come here, Dyana." He patted a spot beside him.

She moved over to lie beside him. The fingers of his left hand curved over her right. Bits of bright sun pierced the canopy of leaves above them and she squinted through lowered lids seeing only green. A private paradise; that was what the small clearing in the New Hampshire woods had become.

Nicholas had driven into the forest until the foot trails became too narrow to maneuver the four-wheeler. They had carried the wicker hamper containing their lunch into woods so thick with towering pine and birch trees they shut out the light and warmth of the summer sun. She spotted scurrying woodland creatures as they came out of their holes to investigate the human intruders, before disappearing in tree trunks or under rotting vegetation. She had been especially intrigued by a tiny brown rabbit that refused to scamper away. It had sat up wiggling its tiny nose and Nicholas said it probably was used to humans because of the numerous camps in the area.

Most of the camps bore Indian names: Hiawatha, Hiwassee Apalachicola and a traditional Berea. The campgrounds bordered lakes or large streams for the campers' swimming and boating activities. Civilization had begun to creep into the area with newer and modern homes alongside the homes which had been there since the turn of the century.

She hadn't understood Lucy's urging for them to combine work with an outdoor outing until Nicholas explained that Dan, Lucy's husband, was due to return home from a business trip in Europe. Lucy's boarders had checked out and she hung out a No Vacancy sign, hoping to spend an uninterrupted day with her frequently absent husband.

"How often does Lucy's husband go abroad?"

"Too often for her," Nicholas replied in a drowsy voice. "But it can't be helped; his position as an importer and exporter of precious stones keeps him crisscrossing the ocean quite a few times during the year."

Dyana turned her head to stare at his profile. "Do you think that's fair to Lucy? She's left with a monumental task of running a large inn with no help."

"Lucy knew that when she married Dan; they were married less than a year ago."

"But that's quite a strain to place on a marriage. Long distance relationships usually don't last."

He sat up, glaring down at her. "Like mine, Dyana?"

If she could've retracted her statement, she would have after seeing the pain on his face. She'd forgotten about his failed marriage. "I wasn't talking about your marriage," she admitted.

Nicholas pulled his knees to his chest, clasping his arms around them. "It wouldn't have survived even if I hadn't gone to Vietnam," he murmured to himself. "Francine and I married for all of the wrong reasons and both of us ended up losing. We were so much alike and too different." His smile was brittle. "It sounds crazy but we wanted the same things but went about achieving them by entirely different means. She wanted fame and all that went with it and . . ."

Dyana sat up, her hand going to his shoulder. "And what?"

A frown creased his forehead as he stared at her hand. "And nothing." The sharp edge in his voice signaled the subject was moot.

She picked up her glass and sipped the wine. Nicholas hadn't loved Francine when he married; he had admitted that to her aunt; but what she didn't understand was why he'd been willing to marry a woman not loving her. Had their marriage been a contract union where each would use the other for financial or business gain? And if it was, what made the deal go sour?

The conversation shifted smoothly when Nicholas recounted his travels to different countries, describing in detail the cities he favored. Vienna, Rome, Hong Kong and Paris had been the ones he returned to as a tourist many times. But she was surprised when he revealed that the States were special to him because it had taken almost sixteen years of his life to discover what made the United States the most talked about, sought-after nation in the world. To him, being born a U.S. citizen had not made him feel quite the citizen until he was able to place his feet firmly on its soil.

The wine, heat and solitude enveloped them as the day slipped quietly into early twilight where they noticed a flitting firefly, and it was with reluctance that they ended their celebration. They retreated from their private world as they walked back to where the Jeep was parked.

The inn was strangely silent when they entered to put away the remains of the picnic. Dyana rinsed and stacked dishes and flatware in the dishwasher while Nicholas put up a pot of coffee.

"Now, don't you two look like the perfect couple." Lucy was smiling from ear to ear. "All you need, Nicky, is an apron and you could pass for a completely domesticated male."

Dyana turned, hoping he wouldn't catch her smiling behind the terry towel. He took several steps toward Lucy. "You're looking for it, Lucille."

Lucy stomped her foot. "Don't you dare call me that! And you'd better not come any closer. I can't have you swinging me around in my condition."

"What condition?"

An attractive flush stained her cheeks. "I'm pregnant. The baby's due early next spring."

Nicholas ran his fingers over her face. "Why didn't you say something before?"

"Tell you before I had the opportunity to tell Dan he was going to be a father?"

Nicholas gathered her to his body, her head coming only to his chest. "Of course not. Congratulations."

Dyana extended her congratulations, feeling left out when she observed their closeness. Lucy teased, ordered him about, hugged and kissed him freely whereas she still hadn't allowed herself that freedom. He'd kissed her twice and both times she knew he had held back. It was as if he'd been waiting; waiting for her to tear down the wall she had erected six years before.

"Good night, Nicholas. Thank you for a wonderful day."

Nicholas braced an arm over her head when she leaned against the door to her bedroom. His eyes photographed every inch of her face before he leaned over, his body never touching hers and kissed her mouth. He stepped closer until both of his hands were anchored on either side of her head, their bodies only inches apart. She wanted to get closer, touch him.

"Good night, sweetheart." He smiled and walked across the hall to his room, leaving her mouth parted and her staring at the closed door.

Days and nights became one. Dyana wrote for Kira and Nicholas edited Carl's character and the narration. She found his writing style very different from the Nicholas Bradshaw he'd shown her and she wondered if this was the real Nicholas. His characters were so human that the reader could smell the fear, feel the blood pumping in their veins and experience the pain of failure and rejection. This is what Michael had been talking about when he told her to pay attention to his writing and she would understand the man.

They had been in New Hampshire for eight days and she felt as if she knew Carl Murphy. Closing her eyes, she could visualize his raven black hair, dark eyes and the frustration when his injured leg wouldn't allow him to play basketball with his sons.

The pages coming out of the laser printer piled up until the finished product numbered nearly eight hundred. She didn't want the project to end because it meant not sharing dinners with Nicholas or having him kiss her when he left her at her bedroom. The last few times she'd surprised him when she rose on tiptoe to kiss him before he'd leaned over to kiss her. Her kissing him gave her an excuse of holding him to maintain her balance.

It was mid-afternoon when they prepared for their return trip and Lucy met them, pale and weak from a bout of nausea. Dan had hired a woman to clean and manage the inn until after the baby was born, overriding his wife's protests.

"Take care of yourself and that baby," Nicholas said, hugging her.

A normally bubbly Lucy sniffed back tears. "You take care, too. And don't take so long to come back for a visit, Nicky." She pressed a kiss to his lips. "Take care you don't let her get away," she hissed with a return of spirit.

It was Dyana's turn to hug and kiss her hostess. "Thanks for everything, Lucy. Good luck with the baby."

Lucy smiled through her tears. "Don't let him get away," she whispered for her ears only. "He deserves the happiness I know you can give him."

"Well, well, girlfriend. I see you managed to get some sun and you look as satisfied as George after your aunt has fed him. How was your week with Mr. Nicholas Bradshaw?"

"Stop being nosy and leave her alone," Susie ordered, frowning at Livvy. "Can't you see the child's tired? She didn't get in until late last night and you're here earlier than ever to interrogate her."

"It's all right, Aunt Susie. If I don't tell her she'll haunt me. We critiqued and edited a manuscript."

"And?"

She shrugged her shoulders, spreading her hands palms up. "That's it, Livvy."

Livvy looked disappointed. "Is that all you did?" she asked with an incredulous look on her face.

Susie stopped her bustling around the kitchen. "If she did anything else and told you about it, I'd put her over my knee and warm up the seat of her pants. Mind your business for the last time."

Livvy stood up in a huff. "That's it. That's the last time I'm going to allow myself to be insulted in this household."

Susie gave her a saccharine smile. "Good-bye, Olivia."

Livvy picked at her curls, pouting. "I'll talk to you later, Dyana." She ignored Susie when she stalked out of the kitchen.

Susie sat down at a bowl filled with green beans and began snapping the ends off. She gave her niece a wary look, trying unsuccessfully to concentrate on the beans. "What happened between you and Nicholas?" she asked, the words rushing out.

"You're as bad as Livvy," Dyana sputtered. "What makes you think something happened?"

Susie sucked her teeth. "I'm not so old I can't see the looks you two give each other. I've never seen anyone drink that much coffee in my life. After the third cup I saw right through him; he didn't want to leave."

"Nicholas drinks coffee by the gallon," Dyana refuted.

"In a pig's eye, Dyana Randolph. The man was falling

asleep on his feet yet he sits here for two hours talking about what I can't remember. Half of what he said sounded foreign to me."

Dyana had to agree with her aunt. The return trip had taken nearly seven hours and Nicholas appeared as reluctant as she'd been for it to end. In two days they would return to the magazine offices and everything that had happened over the past week would become a memory.

"I suppose he's pretty excited about this book we worked on. It's going to be a blockbuster once it's in print and I'm willing to predict the shock waves will be felt from Washington to the Kremlin."

"Politics and spies, huh?"

"Something like that." She took a handful of beans and began snapping the ends. "Did Michael come over to keep you company?"

Susie stirred uneasily in her chair. "He was over Sunday, Monday and Tuesday. It seems as if he couldn't get enough of my cooking," she admitted, looking somewhat embarrassed.

Dyana's hands stopped and she leaned forward to peer closely at her father's twin sister. Her eyebrows inched up in surprise. "He was here three days in a row?"

"Yes." She didn't raise her eyes.

"Isn't that interesting," Dyana mumbled, smiling to herself.

Michael kissed her cheek when she opened the door. He looked her over with a critical eye.

"Going away with Nick appears to agree with you," he concluded.

Dyana laid a hand on his belly. "Keep eating my aunt's cooking and you'll need a new wardrobe."

Michael coughed, pulling at the hair over his ear. "The woman's food is addictive. I'm hooked."

"Michael!" squawked the noisy parrot when Susie called out Michael's name.

"Why you're early," Susie declared when she walked into

the living room. She was still wearing the becoming dress she'd worn to church earlier that morning. "I haven't had time to change."

"Don't. Please," Michael insisted when his eyes examined her full figure. "It looks lovely on you, Susan."

"Why thank you, Michael," Susie gushed.

Dyana looked at her aunt, then Michael. Was something going on that she hadn't been aware of?

"Would you like something to drink before dinner is served, Michael?" Susie asked.

"If you made your delicious lemonade, yes."

"Rest yourself and I'll get it."

Dyana sat in the living room with Michael, wondering why every Sunday was a repeat of the one before. Aunt Susie always asked Michael the same questions and his responses were the same.

Michael removed his jacket and tie, laying both of them on the back of the sofa. Dyana watched as he settled himself on the cushion. Somehow she never saw him as a grandfather or a father figure either; he was her friend. He was someone she could talk to without fear of being criticized. If Michael didn't agree with her, he voiced his reasons and concern; he offered the support she needed without the overpowering protectiveness exhibited by her parents and brothers. He and Susie permitted her the independence she'd always wanted.

"How was New Hampshire?"

"Quaint and beautiful. It was everything you'd imagine it would be: narrow cobblestone streets, covered bridges, pine-covered mountains and churches with tall white spires."

"How many hours a day did you and Nick put in to complete the manuscript?"

"An average of ten to twelve hours," she replied, not disclosing the day both of them had taken off for their "celebration."

Michael smiled. "That sounds like Nick. The man's a workaholic. Didn't he allow you a break?"

"We did take a day off," she admitted. "But once we began it was almost impossible to put it down. I went to bed reliving scenes and there were nights I couldn't get to sleep because my brain was still in high gear."

Susie came into the living room carrying a tray filled with a pitcher of lemonade and two glasses. Michael stood up quickly to take the tray from her hands and set it down on the coffee table. He poured a glass for Dyana, then filled one for himself. He waited until Susie sat before retaking his seat beside her.

"I was asking Dyana about her work with Nick."

Susie smoothed out the voile apron covering the lemon-yellow dress sprigged with delicate violets. "You should've seen the poor kids when they got back Friday night. Nicholas was so tired he couldn't keep his eyes open. He drank coffee until it was coming out of his ears. I don't know why he came all the way down here just to turn around and drive back home. From what he told me, he has more than enough room in his house for Dee to stay over. He could've brought her back on Saturday."

"It's not proper for a young single woman to stay at a man's house, Susan," Michael declared, frowning.

Susie snorted under her breath. "That was in our day, Michael. Nowadays these young people do just about everything they're big enough to do, and that includes trial marriage and parenthood."

"It still doesn't make it right," Michael insisted stubbornly.

"I'm not saying it does, but it happens," Susie returned.

Michael looked at Dyana. "I look at Dyana no differently than I would my own daughter, and I wouldn't want her staying with Nick without a chaperone."

"What's wrong with him?" Susie questioned, bristling.

Michael glared at Susie. "He's no choirboy, Susan."

"What man is?" she retorted hotly.

Michael tugged at the hair over his ear in an unconscious gesture. "I suppose you're right about that, Susan," he conceded. He glanced over at Dyana who seemed to be enjoying the interchange. "I don't want her hurt, that's all."

"She's my flesh and blood and I certainly don't want anything or anyone to hurt her either."

Dyana couldn't believe it. Michael and her aunt were arguing. The tension was there; repressed, but there.

"I have no reason to stay with Nicholas so I don't know why you're fighting."

Michael glanced over at Susie, offering a weak smile. "I'm not fighting with Susan. I only want the best for you, Dyana."

"And I will have the best, Michael," she stated, not understanding this new attitude to protect her.

"I'll see to that," Susie mumbled, pushing to her feet to stand up. "Excuse me while I check on the chicken."

"Why are you fighting with my aunt?" she asked Michael when they were alone.

"The woman's too opinionated."

"So are you."

"But she's worse. If it's not her way, it's no way."

Dyana had to smile. "I think it's a case of too much togetherness. Sundays are enough; don't push your luck with trying for more."

Michael raised his glass, nodding in agreement. "I suppose you're right. I think I'll stick to Sunday dinner." He took a swallow of the lemonade. "Now, about the manuscript. What did you do with it?"

"Nicholas printed two copies. One he sent to Paul by courier and the other he sent to Carl Murphy's wife. He wanted Paul to read it before he meets with him tomorrow."

"I don't know how Nick does it, but he must have a fairy godmother. Everything he touches turns to gold. Murphy's book is what *Pinnacle* needs to compete with the other literary organs. Perhaps he'll consider doing a serial condensation where it'll run for the October and November or November and December issues. I can just see people waiting at the newsstands for a copy."

Dyana closed her eyes, trying to imagine the hype when

the issue of the magazine hit the stands. Her name would not appear anywhere on the printed pages, but knowing she'd contributed to the completion of Carl Murphy's story of blackmail and a coverup within the government's intelligence agency was reward enough.

Nicholas eliminated references which could prove harmful to the country's national security, substituting facts he'd gleaned from his close association with Carl.

"How did you and Nick get along?"

A slow, secret smile touched her mouth. "Well enough to complete editing and typing a two-hundred-thousand word manuscript in a little more than a week."

What she wanted to tell Michael was that working with Nicholas had allowed her to open up to her feelings. Relating Steven's rejection forced her to relive the incident without the torment she always experienced whenever she thought of it. Even his written missive explaining that at age thirty he felt he'd been too young to make a serious commitment to one woman no longer bothered her. Now perhaps Livvy would stop lecturing her when she decided to date some of the men who had expressed an interest in seeing her.

"That's not what I'm talking about and you know it, Dyana," Michael snapped, his voice rising in annoyance.

"He was a perfect gentleman, Michael. Remember, I'm not his type. Nicholas Bradshaw will only date a model, recording star or actress."

"You're an unbelievable woman, Susan Randolph," Michael stated, swallowing a mouthful of baked macaroni. "You sew, cook and probably sing like an angel."

"How would you know about my singing? You've never been to church to hear me sing."

"Invite me, Susan, and I'll come."

"The Lord's house is open to all who want to enter. You don't need my special invitation, Michael Dalton."

Michael raised sad-looking eyes from the plate filled with roast chicken, green beans and baked macaroni and stared at Susie. "Then I'll be here early next Sunday to escort you to church and hear you sing."

Throughout the meal Dyana looked for signs which indicated Michael was interested in more than Susie's cooking. Her meal went untouched as she listened to their conversation.

"Something wrong with your plate, Dyana?"

Susie's voice broke into her trance. "No ma'am. Everything's fine." Lowering her head, she picked up her fork to begin eating.

The meal completed and the dishes washed and put away, Dyana retreated to her bedroom. She did what she normally did on Sunday evenings: she called her parents, manicured her nails and read for several hours before preparing for bed.

Sleep was elusive; it had been for the past two nights. She missed seeing Nicholas and having him kiss her before she retired for bed. And it was the first time in a long time that she missed the companionship of a younger man. She had almost forgotten how to flirt, dance and have someone make her feel desirable. Her past was the past and she was ready to take on the future. But there was only one man who came to mind when she thought of her future: Nicholas Bradshaw.

SIX

Dyana kept her eyes on her hands grasping the pole tightly as the subway car rocked and roared through the tunnel. She was hoping to avoid the leering grin of the man standing opposite her. She'd responded to his good morning but desired no further conversation. But each time she glanced up she saw teeth.

"You have beautiful hands, Miss. Piano fingers," he continued. "Do you play piano?"

"Yes." She didn't bother to look up.

His grin grew wider. "I knew it. I've been watching you for a long time and . . ."

The train stopped short, passengers falling and grabbing for something to hold on to. The lights dimmed and Dyana shouldered her way to the other side of the car to stand near a door. The car remained dark until it pulled into the Fifty-ninth Street station and she escaped quickly, losing the man with the toothy grin in the crowd that swelled out on the platform. Riding the subway wasn't something she'd missed while working in New Hampshire.

It was early and she decided to walk the length of Fifty-ninth Street across Columbus Circle to the east side. The numb ache in her knee could only be worked out with exercise and a pair of low heel shoes and a walk would be the cure.

Joggers and bikers entered and exited Central Park, dodging pedestrians and cars. Yellow taxis swerved in and out of traffic, dispatching and picking up passengers who stood dangerously in the flow of oncoming vehicles. Raucous curses rose above the roar of engines when a cabbie maneuvered to cut off another and Dyana smiled, shaking her head. This was New York City and she loved it.

"Is it really you, Dyana?"

"Very funny, Inez."

"What do you expect? You've been away for weeks . . ."

"A week, Miss Cruz."

Inez Cruz shook a head covered with black shining curls. "No muchacha. You were out for four days," she began counting on her fingers. "Then you come back and stay for an hour before taking off with Nicholas Bradshaw for another week. Now that adds up to two weeks." She looked her over closely. "A little suntan and a satisfied look in your eyes says it all, muchacha."

Dyana caught a flash of brightness on the left hand of the woman who shared the office and gasped loudly. "You're engaged?"

Inez placed her left hand over her chest. "Thought you would never notice."

Dyana threw her arms around Inez, kissing her cheek. "I'm so happy for you."

Inez's eyes shimmered with happy tears. "Oh, Dyana, you don't know how I wanted to share this with you." She pulled back, wiping away the moisture. "For the past two years you've listened to me cry about not knowing whether Jorge loved me enough to want to make me his wife and when it happens you're not here. I wanted you to be the first to know outside of my family."

"I wish you all the happiness you deserve. We'll celebrate over lunch or dinner. Whatever you want," she added, feeling Inez's joy.

"Dyana, Mr. Scranton would like to see you in his office."

She stared at the telephone. She'd been in the office for less than ten minutes and already she was being summoned to meet with the publisher.

Inez smiled. *El jefe* calls. It must be nice to rub shoulders with the rich and powerful."

Dyana secured her handbag in the bottom drawer of her

desk and left to see what Paul Scranton wanted of her. His secretary smiled at her when she knocked on the door and pushed it open.

She dismissed Paul sitting behind his desk when her gaze fell on Nicholas as he sat on a chair beside the desk. He rose to his feet and she was transfixed by his presence. His tawny coloring, tanned to a deep golden brown by the sun, was the perfect foil for a peach-colored shirt and pale wheat light-weight suit. A paisley print tie in brown, peach and jade blended tastefully with the rest of his outfit. He had removed his jacket and she smiled when she saw the dark brown suspenders stretched over his broad chest. Somehow she'd always thought suspenders belonged on old, potbelly men, not on a virile young man. His appearance shocked her after the week in which he'd worn tight faded jeans, tee shirts and tattered footwear.

"Good morning, Dyana. We'll sit over there." Paul pointed to an area in the corner of the office where two love seats sat on an Oriental rug. A low table in blue-veined marble held a flowering cactus plant and the thick bundle she recognized as the Murphy manuscript.

"Hello again," Nicholas whispered as his fingers curved under her elbow to lead her across the large room. He seated her and moved over to sit opposite her, leaving Paul to choose her love seat or his. "May I get you some coffee?"

She smiled, trying to remember how many cups of coffee she'd seen him drink in the week they'd worked together. "Yes."

"How about you, Paul? Coffee?"

Paul sat down next to Dyana, running a hand over his face. "Thanks, Bradshaw."

Paul Scranton was exhausted. The puffiness under his eyes, stooped posture and slow movements said it all. He leaned back, resting his head against the cushioned softness of the love seat and loosened his tie.

Dyana watched Nicholas as he moved over to a credenza to pour coffee from an urn. He balanced two cups, handing one to her and placing Paul's on the table.

"What about yours?" she asked when he retook his seat.

Gray-green eyes brightened with amusement. "I'm trying to cut down on my coffee consumption," he replied, reminding her of Susie's comment about his coffee-drinking marathon abilities.

Paul took a sip of the steaming black brew, grimacing when he burned his tongue. The cup rattled noisily in the saucer when he replaced it on the table. His hand was shaking uncontrollably. "I want to get this over as soon as possible so I can go back home and get some sleep." He trained bloodshot eyes on Dyana. "Bradshaw tells me it was you who wrote for the Kira character."

She looked at Nicholas, her heart pounding wildly. He hadn't mentioned that he was going to tell anyone about her involvement in the manuscript other than that she'd aided with the typing; and when she hadn't typed he did, his fingers skimming the keys even faster than her own eighty words per minute.

"I helped with the characterization."

Nicholas's hand tightened on the arm of the love seat. His eyes darkened to an emerald green, impaling her with their intensity as he sat rigid, glaring at her. "She *wrote* it."

"Let's have it, Dyana," Paul snapped, massaging his temples.

"I wrote it, Paul."

"Now, that wasn't so hard to admit, was it?" Paul gave her a warm smile. "Bradshaw also tells me that you have an idea for a column I should consider. And judging from what I've spent the last couple of nights reading, I agree with him. Get a proposal together, a sample column, and it's yours."

She stared numbly at Paul, then transferred her gaze to Nicholas. His impassive expression revealed nothing. He'd done what Michael said he would do. A week with him had accomplished what she'd hoped for ever since she'd begun her writing career. She had her column!

She sank back against the cushions wishing she were alone so she could laugh, cry or scream out the bubbling excitement. "Thank you." The low, husky expression of gratitude was lost on Paul when he glanced up at his secretary who had entered the office.

"Mrs. Murphy is on the line for Mr. Bradshaw."

"I'll take it here," Nicholas said, rising to take the call.

Nicholas turned his back, staring out through the wall of glass as he held the receiver to his ear. His voice was low, not permitting her or Paul to overhear what was being said. The call lasted less than two minutes when he replaced the receiver on its cradle.

"Carl Murphy's wife is flying in on the noon shuttle to sign the contract."

All signs of fatigue vanished when Paul stood up in one swift motion. "Damn!" he swore savagely. "I forgot to follow up on the contract."

"You what?" The two words exploded from Nicholas.

"I thought I had more time. I had no idea you would finish so quickly."

"Let's get down to business, Paul," Nicholas threatened. "Mrs. Murphy will be here in less than three hours and I expect you to have a contract for her signature and a check she can deposit into her bank. The woman has mortgaged her home, spent her life savings and the money set aside for her sons' college education for her husband's legal defense, and you have the story every publishing house would kill for. Jerk her around and I swear I'll walk out of here to auction it to the highest bidder and leave you looking for an editor for *Pinnacle.*"

"Not so fast, Bradshaw. Remember, you have a contract with Westgate Publishing."

Nicholas picked up his jacket, slipping his arms into the sleeves. "Then sue me!"

"No!" Both men looked at her when she screamed. She hid her hands in the pockets of her dress to hide their shaking. If Nicholas walked out with the manuscript there would be too many losers. Westgate would sue him, *Pinnacle* would lose the Murphy story and she would lose Nicholas. Not once did she think about losing her own column. That was no longer important to her.

"She's right, Bradshaw. We can work this out."

"How?"

Dyana wanted to go to Nicholas and soothe away the tension in his jaw and tell him he couldn't leave; he couldn't leave her. Her eyes traced the curve of his eyebrows, cheekbones, the cleft in his strong chin and firm mouth, committing them to memory. If she was to see him for the last time, this is how she wanted to remember him. Confident, arrogant and uncompromising.

"I'll check with the controller while you go over the contract," Paul suggested.

Nicholas slipped his hands into the pockets of his trousers, leaning against the desk. He was in control and wasn't above letting the publisher know it. "Ronnie expects me to meet her at the airport."

"I'll meet her," Dyana volunteered.

Paul gestured wildly. "It's settled, Bradshaw. Dyana will meet Mrs. Murphy and you and I can tie up the loose ends here."

Nicholas straightened, blinking at her in surprise. "Are you sure you want to do this?"

She nodded. It was the least she could do for him. How could she measure a column against meeting someone at the airport? "Which airport and what does she look like?"

Paul practically ran out of the office, hoping to avoid a debacle. The bicoastal courting of his ex-wife had left him disorganized and out of touch with the comings and goings of his corporation.

Nicholas withdrew a key from his pocket and walked over to put it in her hand, closing her fingers over the metal. "Her flight is coming into LaGuardia, number one sixty-nine, the Eastern shuttle. She's tall, nearly five ten, and she has red hair and lots of freckles. You can't miss her."

Dyana tilted her head to smile up at him. She'd almost forgotten how beautiful he was. She lowered her lids but not before he caught a glimpse of the faraway burning in her eyes. It was a while before he was able to exhale. He released her hand.

"The garage's address is on the key ring. Drive carefully, Dyana."

"I promise."

Once she adjusted to the feel of the powerful sports car she knew why Nicholas drove the Corvette. She was able to pass and take curves with an ease she'd never felt before when driving. When stopping for a light, she drew admiring glances from other drivers and an occasional wolf whistle from truckers. The car's body had been restored to where it looked new.

Midday traffic was light and she arrived at LaGuardia with time to spare. She parked in the short-term lot and checked arrivals for Veronica Murphy's flight.

She thumbed through a magazine, not reading any of the words on the page; she was still too excited about the prospect of having her own column. There was research to do, but on which topic? She had hundreds to consider.

Veronica Murphy was stunning! She was tall and thin, wearing a black silk blouse and linen gabardine slacks. A mane of fiery red hair flowed to her shoulders and as she strode through the terminal, men were openly ogling her.

"Mrs. Murphy?"

Pale green eyes in a face sprinkled with freckles observed her closely before they crinkled with a smile. "Yes."

Dyana extended her hand. "Nicholas Bradshaw asked that I pick you up. He was unable to come himself," she added quickly. "He and the publisher are finalizing the documents necessary for the sale of your husband's book."

Veronica Murphy shook the proffered hand and nodded. "Thank you . . ."

"Dyana. Dyana Randolph."

"If it's Dyana, then you must call me Ronnie. I can't believe all of this is taking place. The money from the book will pay the legal fees for Carl's appeal. Nicholas has been more than a friend to Carl; he's become his salvation. How long have you known Nicholas?" she asked, not pausing to catch her breath.

Dyana led the way to the parking lot, trying to keep up with the redhead's long strides. "Two weeks."

"That's hardly long enough for him to trust you to drive his car," she said. "You must be quite special."

Dyana smiled at Ronnie. "A man and his car."

Ronnie slipped on a pair of sunglasses against the blinding sun. "It's been that way with Nicholas for several years now. Men have to have their toys. For some it's women and for others it's cars. It's been too long since Nicholas has had his head turned by a woman. His divorce was somewhat ugly."

Dyana waited to pull out into the parkway traffic, accelerating until she'd reached the speed limit. "Did you know Nicholas's ex-wife?" she asked.

"I sure did. I was the one who introduced him to Francine. It was the last time I ever attempted to play matchmaker."

Her curiosity was piqued. "What happened?"

Ronnie shifted a red eyebrow behind the dark glasses. "Are you interested in Nicholas?" she asked directly.

What did Ronnie expect her to say? That she was in love with Nicholas Bradshaw and that she wanted to know all there was to know about him before she committed herself? "I have to work with him and I thought you could tell me something about him to make my job easier," she half-lied. She knew how it was to work with him.

Ronnie gave her a long look before replying. "Nicholas is one of the more open and honest men I've ever met, and he expects the same from everyone he deals with. A word of advice: never lie to him, Dyana. Francine lied again and again and whatever they could've salvaged in their marriage was destroyed."

She paused, seemingly groping for the right words. "Nicholas stayed with Carl and I until his divorce was final, and we convinced him to write the book about his experiences in Southeast Asia after he finally got his head together. He was like another person when he began writing, neither Carl nor I recognizing him as the Nicholas we once knew. He moved into a little apartment in Washington, and I'd stop by to find him crying like a child. He would lock himself in the bedroom, refusing to come out. Whenever I saw him like that I fell apart myself. It was years later when he confessed that he had nightmares similar to the ones combat soldiers experienced and he felt as if someone had swallowed his soul, not allowing him to know the difference between good and evil. There were times when he thought the taking of a human life was the right thing to do and at other times he knew it was wrong."

Dyana shivered although the temperature was in the eighties. Nicholas had not been in combat, yet he carried the wounds which had only healed with time. Or had they? He'd achieved fame with *Souls of the Children,* but he also felt the pain and suffering of the innocent souls who were never given the chance to act out their futures.

She pulled Livvy into the room Susie had set up as their library. It was small and homey-looking with back issues of *Ebony* dating to the mid-fifties lining bookshelves. "Come take a look at the calendar I've put together for my column," she urged.

Livvy pulled back, stopping their progress. "You mean to say that you have a column?" she asked, her eyes widening behind the tinted lenses.

Dyana placed her hands on her hips, nodding and smiling. "What you see preening before you, Dr. Olivia Patterson, is the newest assistant editor of *Pinnacle Magazine.*"

Livvy assumed a similar pose and walked around the room, tilting her chin as she looked down her nose. "And whom may I ask is responsible for your good fortune?"

Dyana paused. "The editor."

Livvy stopped her prancing and thrust out her chin. "And pray tell, Miss Randolph, could that editor be the one and only Nicholas Bradshaw?"

Dyana's shoulders slumped, her exuberance waning. "Don't make it sound like that, Livvy."

"Just like that," she said, snapping her fingers, "he decided to approve your column."

Dyana flopped down on a horsehair chair. "He presented it to the publisher and Paul Scranton gave the approval."

"Why do you think he did it, Dyana?"

"What are you trying to say?"

"He may have presented it because he wants something in return."

"Tell me what that would be, please," she retorted, giving Livvy a hostile glare.

Livvy did not seem at all perturbed by her apparent outburst. "You, Dee Randolph. I've met more Nicholas Bradshaws than you could ever count. Some may not be as good-looking or famous, but they all have the same drive. And that is, if they see something they want they don't stop until they're able to obtain it. Your editor will not let anything stand in his way, Dyana. If it means granting your every wish, he'll do whatever it takes to make you happy."

"You know nothing about him! You've only met him once."

"Once is enough, girlfriend. The man's hooked. Those beautiful eyes of his speak volumes. They say things which should not be said in polite company."

"I doubt very much if Nicholas would allow personal feelings to interfere with his professional judgment. If he felt I wasn't capable of writing a column he would've never approached Paul with it." She couldn't disclose any of the details of Carl Murphy's book or her involvement with it.

"Open your eyes, Dyana," Livvy pleaded softly. "Nicholas Bradshaw would write the column himself if he had to. Don't you see how the man looks at you?"

"He looks at me no differently than any other man. I'm not so grotesque that I can't get a little male attention every once in a while," she blurted out, a slight edge in her voice confirming her rising temper.

"Men you refuse to acknowledge as men. How many dates have you turned down since I've known you? Ten, twenty? The word is out that Dee Randolph doesn't like men. No man who has heard of you will come within two feet of you, Dyana. Nicholas is the only man I've seen you laugh with or give that wide-eyed innocent look. The poor man can't help himself when you look at him like that."

"You give me much too much credit, Livvy," she continued, this time in a softer voice. "Nicholas could have any woman he found himself attracted to, and I refuse to believe he's doing this because I flutter my lashes at him. Why me, Livvy? I'm no one special."

"Wrong," Livvy whispered. "You're what Nicholas wants and mark my words, he's going to have you and I promise I won't say that I told you so." Her friend was unaware of the effect she had on men. "Enough about Nicholas. I'm ready to look at the calendar you've developed."

She tried to dispel Livvy's ominous prediction about Nicholas and her reason for him approving her column and was successful when she spread the large calendar out on the desk. She had charted events from every state and several regions in Canada, and the Caribbean she hoped would be of interest to residents and tourists in these areas.

She listed the quaint charm of the Pennsylvania Dutch region, the revival of New York's South Street Seaport, the western route of the Lewis and Clark expedition through the rugged splendor of Nebraska, major archaeological sites in Mexico, the Pablo Casals festival in Puerto Rico, the multicultural charm of New Orleans, the ancient civilization of the Anasazi ruins in the Four Corners of the United States Southwest and more from less-known areas in North America.

Livvy peered closely at the pages covered with small neat print. "You're serious about this, aren't you? There's no way you can cover all of these events and places, Dyana."

"I won't," she laughed. "What I plan to do is compose a form letter to send to all of the visitors' bureaus and local chambers for places of interest and information on what I've noted here. I'm going to request the names and addresses of local historians for that little extra piece of folklore which probably would never appear in most travel guides."

"I suppose there is a method to your madness, girlfriend. Where do you intend to begin this tour?"

"Believe it or not I intend to begin right in our own backyard. My aunt's bookshelves are filled with all of the factual material I'll need to do a column about the famous Apollo Theatre."

"Why the Apollo?"

"Why not the Apollo?" She rolled up the calendar. "It's an institution and the first home to many of today's superstars. The Apollo's back with new faces but the spirit is still the same: people want to be there to discover tomorrow's talented performers. I've pulled out several dozen back issues of *Ebony* to familiarize myself with the performers from the past. Of course I'll contact the present management for an interview."

"Knowing you, you'll get exactly what you want," Livvy said. "You're incredible, girlfriend. Why don't you package whatever you have and sell it, Dee Randolph? There would be a lot more happy women in the world if they could effect your indifference and still get men to fall all over them. I say you're batting a thousand. First Michael and now Nicholas. But there's a difference. Nicholas is not a tired old man. Just be ready for him when he decides he wants you, my friend."

At ten, Dyana and the others who made up the editorial department filed into the conference room for an impromptu meeting. Nicholas had met with Michael and several associate editors earlier that morning when they'd shared a breakfast session. Everyone was anxious to discover why they were being summoned to an unscheduled meeting when in the past they had met bimonthly instead of weekly.

Nicholas glanced down at his watch and stood up. "Ladies, gentlemen, may we begin?" He waited until everyone was seated. "We have a great deal of material to cover this morning and the sooner we begin the more we'll be able to accomplish."

Coffee cups, napkins, pens and pads covered the U-shaped

conference table while all eyes were directed toward Nicholas. Lacing his fingers together, he smiled. "There are big things happening for *Pinnacle* and although I'm not at liberty to disclose any of the facts at this time, I can assure you that everyone will share in the celebrating."

Dyana raised questioning eyebrows when Inez leaned over to ask her what was going on. She ignored the silent glances when eyes shifted in her direction and watched Nicholas put on his glasses to read the items he had written down on a pad. His gaze met hers before he directed his attention to the others seated around the table.

"I've called this meeting this morning to discuss the changes which will influence the look and scope of our magazine. These changes will affect everyone; from the publisher to the mail clerk. We intend to make certain modifications without sacrificing our reputation of publishing the highest quality of literary talent available for our subscribers. Keeping this in mind, I want to attract readers from every ethnic, socioeconomic and geographic group in North America. We intend to do this with more timely and controversial topics. Is there anyone here opposed to this change?"

Asia Beaumont ran her fingers through short, feathered ebony hair and leaned forward to give Nicholas a full view of her generous cleavage rising above the neckline of her dress. She affected a seductive pout as she raised her hand to get his attention.

"We all seem to agree to increasing our readership," she stated in a velvety tone, "but I question whether we should change so much that our long-time subscribers will not recognize their magazine."

Dyana's spine stiffened when she saw a fleeting look of annoyance on Nicholas's face. She'd seen it enough to know what to expect from him.

"Miss Beaumont," Nicholas replied, removing his glasses. "You are entitled to your opinion; however, I need cooperation in this undertaking. All of the senior editors agree with the changes and if you are opposed to working with the others may I suggest you hand in whatever you're currently working on and pick up your check from Aaron."

Asia sat up quickly and Dyana felt sorry for the woman. It was unfortunate that she had to face humiliation before learning that Nicholas was all business when it involved his profession.

"What do you have planned, Nicholas?" asked one of the assistant editors.

"I'd like for us to work more closely with our parent company, Westgate. At least twice a year we should excerpt a potential bestseller, hopefully cashing in on some of the advance sales. This way we're assured of greater profits than we've managed to realize these past few years. Larger profits translate into larger raises, bonuses and a possible profit-sharing package. We'll also expand each issue a possible ten to twelve pages."

"Will these additional pages be used for advertising?"

"Not entirely," Nicholas replied. "We'll be adding at least two new columns. Dyana will be submitting a proposal on something she calls *Regions* and Zack will keep our readers up to date on the financial climate of Wall Street and the world market with a column yet to be named. I've sent letters to writers who've covered crisis situations on both sides of the oceans and I expect pieces covering the complicated religious strife in India, the military activities in Central America, the war against drugs in the Western Hemisphere and an insider's look at the paramilitary groups amassing strength in many regions of the United States. I've checked our letters-to-the-editor files for the past three years, and I've made a list of possible topics some of you might want to cover in your columns. The possibilities are endless: bilingual education, the plight of the homeless, the pandemic increase in corporate raiding, white collar crime and the rampant corruption of elected and appointed officials. I think I've said enough," he concluded. A flash of humor crossed his face when a spattering of applause broke out.

Dyana smiled at Michael when he gave her a thumbs-up

sign and she turned to receive the congratulatory wishes from her peers. Inez was tugging on her arm to get her attention.

"What's going on, muchacha?"

Dyana pulled her close. "I can't tell you. At least not yet. Trust me, Inez."

"I'll think about it," she shot back, laughing.

Michael kissed her cheek, his hands going to her shoulders. "You did it, darling. I knew you would."

She saw Nicholas heading her way and tried to extract herself from his embrace. "No, Michael. Not here."

Nicholas stopped behind Michael and as her eyes met his, she felt a shock go through her when her stomach churned and knotted in anguish. His withering glare spoke the volumes Livvy had noticed; but they didn't say he wanted her. He spun around on his heel, hiding the pain he would not permit her to see.

"Am I going too quickly?"

Dyana glanced up to look at Nicholas for the first time since he'd asked her to come to his office. If he had recovered from Michael's open demonstration of affection she hadn't. She was unable to understand why it bothered her to have Nicholas observe her with Michael whenever he kissed or hugged her. It had never bothered her before. Why now?

"No . . . no. I have everything."

Nicholas pinched the bridge of his nose with the thumb and forefinger of his left hand, staring at her from under lowered lids. Leaning back in the chair, he crossed his arms over a stark white shirt. A yellow tie hung loosely from an opened collar.

"I spoke to Paul and apparently he's decided to waive the condition of your submitting a proposal. I told him you probably needed the time to do your research."

Dyana's head came up quickly. A cry of excitement escaped her mouth before she clamped a hand over it. The gesture delighted Nicholas, and he left his chair to walk around the desk to sit on a corner in front of where she sat staring up at him with eyes that sparkled with joy.

"Thank you," she sighed, lowering her hand.

He grasped her hand tightly, bringing it up to his lips. "It's the least I could do for you, Dee. Especially after what you did for Carl." He lowered his head to place a light kiss on her fingers.

Dyana wanted to jerk her hand away. The heat of his kiss shot up her arm, warming her body and weakening her knees. Closing her eyes, she swayed slightly. Did he know what he was doing to her? Did he not know that everything about him searched deeply to reach inside of her and melt away any shred of resistance she had to allow her to give him all she had; and that was her love. She pulled her hand away, moving back.

She couldn't. She couldn't fall in love with him. Everything about him was so right and it was so wrong. It was as if her life had become an instant replay. First Steven and now Nicholas.

"What's the matter, darling?" Nicholas saw the haunted look in her eyes and her trembling hands.

"Don't call me that!"

His fingers bit into the tender flesh on her arms. "Why?" His hot breath seared her moist face.

It was over in a flash. She swallowed down her fear, breathing heavily as if she'd run a grueling race. "I'm all right, Nicholas," she sighed, giving him a small smile.

A worried frown left his smooth forehead and he released her, not believing that she was all right. "Are you sure?" She nodded. "Well, if that's the case, I'd like to know if you would come with me to a ball game tonight. The Mets and Phillies."

She wanted to refuse, but it had been years since she'd been to a game. Living with four brothers exposed her to baseball, football, basketball and any other televised sport at an early age.

Nicholas reached into the breast pocket of his shirt, withdrawing two tickets. "Box seats, behind first base," he crooned, waving them under her nose. "Don't you want to see me go crazy when the home boys wallop the Phillies?"

Her slim fingers caught his thick wrist. "You're on. But you're wrong about the Mets beating the Phillies, Mr. Bradshaw."

Attractive lines fanned out around his eyes. "Want to place a wager, Miss Randolph?"

She gave him a haughty glare. "You set the stakes."

"If the Mets win you'll have to go out with me every weekend for a month," he said quickly, watching the surprised expression on her lovely face.

It could've been worse, she thought. Much worse. She bit down on her lower lip trying to think of a comparable wager.

"I'm waiting, Dyana."

"Don't harass me, Nicholas. I'm thinking." The trouble was she couldn't think. "Okay. I've got it. If the Phillies win, then you'll have to take me to a concert or play of my choice."

"Shake," he demanded, extending his hand.

Her hand was swallowed up in his and she felt no matter who won, she and Nicholas would both be winners.

Fingernails bit into the flesh of her palms and she chewed her lower lip mercilessly, ignoring the pain as she was caught up in the tension-filled game. Her eyes were glued on the pitcher and batter, ignoring the triumphant smile on Nicholas's face. Popcorn and peanut shells crackled under the soles of her shoes and she waved away the cup of soda Nicholas held out to her.

"Leave me alone," she hissed through clenched teeth. "You're breaking my concentration."

Nicholas draped an arm around her shoulders. "It's too late for hexes, sweetheart. Admit defeat," he shouted to be heard above the roar of the capacity crowd.

The chant of "Let's go, Mets" shook Shea Stadium from the upper level to the playing field. Mets fans were looking for the victory which would put their team in first place. The

Phillies' 4–0 lead had vanished when the Mets catcher blasted a fast ball over the left field wall to clear the bases. A large red apple went up and down another two times, when with two outs there were back-to-back homers allowing the Mets to establish a 7–4 lead over the Phillies. Now it was the top of the ninth and the Phillies were down to their last out.

"You're really enjoying this, aren't you?" she asked Nicholas. She smiled up at him when he stood along with the other fifty plus thousand fans to stomp and cheer their team. His shirt was rumpled and hung out of the waistband of his slacks while the odor of stale beer clung to his shoulders where he had been showered by an overzealous fan several rows behind them.

His arm slipped lower to her waist to pull her against the solid hardness of his thigh. "I'm going to enjoy collecting my wager much more than this game."

A loud groan went up when the batter walked. Nicholas sat, pulling her down with him and she rested her head against his shoulder. She was tired, but she couldn't remember the last time she had had so much fun. She was wearing her opposing team's sweatshirt, but didn't care because it kept out the strong winds sweeping across the ballpark. Nicholas had left his suit jacket in the car and when she began to rub her bare arms against the night air, he went in search of a concession stand to bring back the shirt, heralding the 1986 World Series Championship. He'd spread it out across his chest to taunt her with it before she took it and slipped it over her dress.

"I concede defeat," she mumbled.

"And I accept it most humbly."

The next batter lined to the first baseman and the game was over. Everyone stood to leave, clapping and singing to the familiar victory song, "Celebration" by Kool and the Gang.

Nicholas held her hand tightly as they shuffled along the ramps and out into the parking fields. It was another twenty minutes before they inched their way to the parkway for the ride back to Manhattan.

Twinkling lights from the Triborough Bridge and towering apartment buildings lit up the skyline like a sparkling diamond on soft black velvet. Nicholas switched on the radio to a station which featured light, relaxing music and adjusted the heat.

"It was fun, Nicholas. Thanks for asking me."

He glanced over at her delicate profile. The brisk wind had swept her hair around her face and his fingers tightened on the steering wheel to prevent their brushing the sunstreaked strands away from her silken cheek.

"Would you like doing it again?"

"Yes." She pressed back against the seat, closing her eyes. "When do you intend to start collecting on your bet?"

"Friday night." He glanced over his right shoulder to change lanes. "Friday night we'll have dinner out after work. Saturday night we'll go to a supper club for a blues show only blocks from where you live and Sunday . . ."

"Saturday and Sunday?" She sat up, suddenly alert. "What are you talking about?"

"The wager was you would go out with me every weekend for a month."

"I understand the wager, Nicholas. You said every weekend, not every night."

"What is the weekend, Dyana? Is it not Friday, Saturday and Sunday," he said, answering for her. "Webster says it's the period from Friday night or Saturday to Monday morning."

Her hands went to her hips. "And you intend to take it literally?"

"I do," he stated, giving her a quick glance. "And there's no need to get into a huff about it. I won't keep you out too late. I wouldn't want you to get circles under those lovely eyes." He smiled when she turned her back. "Do you like foreign films, darling? There is a little theater in Greenwich Village which features foreign films with English subtitles I'd like to take you to. Another time we'll tour Chinatown, Little Italy and take a ride on the ferry to the Statue of Liberty."

"Take a walk, Nicholas Bradshaw."

He laughed. The rich, unrestrained sound made her smile in spite of his double talk. "We'll have fun, Dyana," he promised when he saw her shoulders shake with laughter.

SEVEN

Susie perched the half-moon glasses on the end of her nose as she examined her handiwork. "I must say this one is my finest creation to date. What do you think, Dee?"

"It's beautiful, Aunt Susie," Dyana replied, not bothering to look up from what she was reading. "Who's it for?"

Susie measured the width of her niece's shoulders with a professional eye. "I don't know."

"Why did you make it?"

Susie's glasses swung from the gold chain around her neck to rest on her full bosom. "I did it on a whim."

Dyana raised her head, pushing aside the book to stare at an exquisite dress in ivory organza. Her aunt had designed a wedding gown with a lowered Sabrina neckline and a fili-gree of Alençon lace. It was a gown for a summer wedding with pouf sleeves, a scalloped hem and chapel train. She rose from the chair to walk slowly toward the garment stretched over the dress form.

"You did this on a whim?" she asked, fingering the lace. Her eyes met her aunt's. "Why?"

Susie removed the pincushion attached to her wrist with a length of elastic and the tape measure from her neck and replaced them in a large wicker sewing basket. "I guess I had nothing to do and I had to keep my hands busy."

"But you don't make samples, Aunt Susie," Dyana in-sisted. "I've never known you to make a dress without some-one commissioning you to sew it."

"Well, I did and that's it!"

Dyana was stunned. She'd never known her aunt to raise her voice at her. What was going on? First Michael acts as if he wants to be her father; Livvy lectures her on Nicholas's ulterior motive for having Paul approve her getting a column and now her aunt gets testy with her when she asks her about doing something completely out of character.

Everyone was crazy—everyone except she and Nicholas. She'd recovered from Tuesday's late night at Shea Stadium to make it into the office on time the following morning, but didn't get the opportunity to see too much of Nicholas because he'd scheduled meetings with different departments all week and it wasn't until Friday night when he took her to an Armenian restaurant in the Thirties that they were able to recapture their easygoing camaraderie.

She'd allowed him to order for her and was pleased with his selection of a spicy roast lamb in a yogurt sauce. As he'd promised, she was home before nine. He'd brushed her lips with a feathery kiss and whistled off-key as he strolled the length of the hall and went out of the brownstone building.

"I'm going to get ready for my date," she said to her aunt's back. Susie continued rearranging the contents of her sewing basket, not acknowledging her.

Nicholas had arrived and she still could not decide on what to wear. Slacks, blouses and dresses covered her bed. Her wardrobe was endless; her aunt made everything she wore except for her jeans and swimwear. She chewed a fingernail, frowning when she chipped the color off the tip. The color was a soft pumpkin orange and she knew it was too late to change her polish and that eliminated anything in red or pink.

She eyed a dark green silk shirtwaist. She'd only worn it once before. The color was good; it reminded her of the color of Nicholas's eyes. She pulled it over her head and buttoned the pleated bodice and slipped the matching belt through the loops around her tiny waist, smoothing out the slightly flaring skirt. It definitely was something she should wear to work, not a supper club, but it was too late to change. Two inches of black patent heels and a pair of large jade and onyx earrings dressed it up a little.

Mascara, shadow and orange lipstick. She thrust her face

in the mirror, wrinkling her nose. "You're too old for this," she told her reflection. Worrying about what to wear and if Nicholas would be pleased with how she looked was insane. He had to like her or why else would he see her so often, especially since she was neither a model nor an actress.

Nicholas was reading from several printed pages to Susie and neither of them glanced her way when she walked into the living room. He was clothed entirely in black: an unconstructed open jacket, a silky shirt buttoned to the neck and a pair of loose-fitting slacks and Italian loafers. She let out a sigh; she was not overdressed.

Susie was enthralled, her mouth compressed as she hung on to his every word. Golden eyes were fixed on his lowered head as behind his reading glasses Nicholas's eyes raced across the pages.

" 'It was over; both of us knew it. Kira sat, huddled in the corner, hiding from the world. A single tear was squeezed from the corner of one eye and trailed down an alabaster cheek. She would not let out her fear or grief. It was as if she couldn't allow herself to lose control. It always had been that way. She showed me only what she wanted me to see, but I managed to see beyond the wall. I saw a woman who'd lived for years denying what she was actually feeling. To exhibit these feelings meant not being strong, and to her being strong was everything. She'd weakened only once when she spoke of the man whom she trusted more than her father. I felt jealous of this faceless, nameless monster who'd stolen the only thing this lonely, malleable creature had to give: love. Did I want her love? Oh, yes! I wanted it more than I wanted life, and I feared for my life. Giving up my life meant giving up my family, while she had nothing to give up. She reached out to me, the tiny hand with a network of delicate blue veins trembling. Baxter stepped between us, blocking her from view. I closed my eyes to hide my tears and when I gathered enough courage to raise my head, she was gone. I still remember a single tear, trembling and silent. It will haunt me to my grave.' "

"Oh, how sad," Susie whispered. "What happened to them, Nicholas?"

Nicholas continued to stare at the printed words on the page. "They're both in prison."

"That's a pity. I try only to read books with a happy ending," she said. "If it's sad, I leave it alone."

Nicholas stared across the room at Dyana. "You may not have a choice because what I just read was written by your niece."

Susie turned, following his gaze. "Dee?"

Dyana felt as if she'd been stripped bare. Nicholas had asked her to write the scene where Carl and Kira had been allowed to see each other for the last time before their trial and she'd voiced her reluctance because it reminded her too much of another time in her own life. It was only with his gentle urging that she paralleled the scene with that of her leaving Philadelphia and all of the bitter memories.

She forced a smile. "If you listen to Nicholas he'll tell you that I wrote the entire book."

Nicholas rose to his feet, looking powerful and formidable in the black attire. He winked at Susie. "It'll take time for her to overcome her modesty."

Dyana bit back the words threatening to fall from her tongue. It was Carl Murphy's story and she didn't want to be associated with a convicted spy even if he was a close friend of Nicholas Bradshaw.

"How could you read that to her?" she ranted. Nicholas tightened his grip on her hand tucked into the bend of his arm when she tried pulling away. "I can't remember when I've been so embarrassed. What made you do that?"

"Are you finished, Dyana?" he asked softly.

Heat flooded her face and she felt like a chastised child. "I'm finished."

Nicholas stopped under a streetlight. The fingers of his right hand curved under her jaw to tilt her chin. The light threw shadows across his face, distorting the planes and hollows of his cheekbones.

"It's time you faced reality, Dyana. You're a beautiful and talented woman and the time for hiding is over. You must learn to accept the accolades as well as the deprecation." His fingers slipped around her neck to pull her head to his shoulder. "It's the praise that keeps you going when something you think is good flops. I've been there, darling," he rasped against her ear. "I've hit the highs and the lows and trust me, the highs are always better."

Her arms slipped around his waist inside of the jacket as she laid her cheek to his chest and counted the steady strong beats of his heart. Her senses were filled with him as her emotions spun out of control. Who was he? This man who made her laugh, who guided her and encouraged her to become the best she could be? How was he able to make her forget that any other man existed? Trembling, she melted against him. He was Nicholas Bradshaw, the man she'd fallen in love with.

Sutton's Supper Club was only blocks from where she lived, and although she passed it each time she took the subway, this was the first time she'd been inside.

It was small, intimate and its warmth enveloped them as soon as they were greeted by their hostess. She and Nicholas pressed their cheeks together and Dyana could not ignore the jealousy tightening her chest.

The woman shook back a wealth of beaded, braided hair, smiling. "It's been a while, Nicky. What brings you out of the sticks?"

"All work and no play makes John a dull boy, Aziza."

"Even if you were named John, you would never be dull," the woman Nicholas had called Aziza crooned.

"Aziza, this is Dyana. Dyana, Aziza."

Both women eyed each other, then smiled to exchange polite greetings. Aziza led them to a table against a wall lined with mirrors.

Dyana slid gracefully into the chair Nicholas held out for her wondering if he knew any unattractive women. Aziza's braided hair showed off the smoothness and deep rich dark brown color of her oval face to its best advantage, highlighting the deep-set black eyes gleaming like polished jet. Large hammered silver shields hung from her lobes, offsetting three sets of silver studs along the upper portion of her ears.

"What would you like to drink, sweetheart?" he asked.

"Tonic with lime." It was the first thing she could think of.

"Make that two," Nicholas told Aziza.

"What does her name mean?" Dyana asked when they were alone.

"She told me it means 'beautiful' in Swahili."

"And that she is," Dyana mumbled, focusing on a black and white print on a wall above his head.

"That's a matter of one's taste."

"You don't think she is?" she asked, staring at him.

"Whether I think she is or isn't doesn't matter, Dyana. It only matters what I think of you." He moved a small glass containing a burning candle away from the center of the table and covered her hand with his. "I'm a very old-fashioned guy," he replied in a quiet tone. "I believe in having only one woman; one at a time. I've never been able to play head games. I've seen what it can do to a person. It can be self-destructive."

His face clouded with sad memories and Dyana wondered if his pain had been so deep that it wouldn't allow him to trust another woman.

"We all carry scars, darling," he said in a low velvet voice. Sighing heavily, he closed his grip on her hand. "What saved me was that I married a woman I did not love. Carl married Ronnie after seeing her off and on for several years. Both of them decided I should sample wedded bliss and that's when Ronnie introduced me to a girl she'd roomed with when they were modeling. I took Francine out a few times and we talked about what we wanted for our futures. I wanted to be a James van der Zee and Ansel Adams. I didn't want to be good; I wanted to be the best and Francine was the first woman I'd met who understood my drive to be successful because she wanted the same.

"She was modeling, taking singing and acting lessons and her agent had billed her as the next Dorothy Dandridge.

Working for *Life* kept me busy and away most of the time. I didn't mind the traveling as much as the coming home. The loneliest feeling in the world is stepping off a plane and having no one meet you. I returned to Dulles one night after a twenty-hour flight from India and saw Francine waiting for me. She'd called the magazine and was told when my flight was due to arrive. I married her the next week."

Dyana was transfixed by his wistful expression and his caressing voice. She tried to comprehend that he'd married a woman out of gratitude. He needed and Francine had fulfilled that need.

Pain tightened his jaw and hardened his eyes. "I accepted the assignment to photograph what was going on in Vietnam and Francine begged me not to leave her. She refused to understand what this assignment meant to me and she said I would live to regret accepting it."

"Did you?" she whispered.

He drew his full lower lip between his teeth, staring through her with those electric green eyes of his. "No," he practically growled. "Only because it allowed me to see what kind of a woman I had committed my future to. It appears as if she wasn't above doing what she had to do to further her career. The names of the men she'd been with read like signatures on the Constitution. I initiated the divorce action and she contested it. I didn't want to hurt her but my lawyer subpoenaed her lovers and the rest was history. Most of these men had wives of their own and after a while no agent or producer would let her through the front door or accept a call from anyone who represented her."

Dyana felt an empathy for Francine. She had embarked on a mission she had no chance of winning. She'd wanted it all—Nicholas and her career—and lost them both.

"Here you are, folks." Aziza placed their drinks on the table along with a small plate filled with cheese, crackers and fruit. Her beaded braids swayed like a screen. "A buffet will be served in about forty-five minutes. Enjoy!"

Dyana took a sip of the drink, shaking off the somber mood created by Nicholas's disclosures about his ex-wife.

She was swept into a soothing, melancholy mood created by the quartet playing the slow rhythmic sound of blues. A keyboard player, guitarist, drummer and sax player pumped out throbbing renditions of "Danny Boy," "The Dark Side of the Street" and Billie Holiday's "God Bless the Child." The words were sad, sung with a true heartbreaking quality and the patrons nodded as if they knew exactly what the lead singer was trying to convey.

She glanced at Nicholas and saw a mysterious smile curving his sensuous mouth when the drummer went into a monologue about going off to war and returning to find his girl married to his best friend. He crooned about pain so deep that he wanted to return to the battlefield where an enemy bullet would put him out of his misery. The patrons laughed when he ended by saying the woman had not a faithful bone in her body because when the friend was arrested for operating an illegal still, his wife ran off with the revenue agent. Her reputation became legend throughout Mississippi for leaving a trail of broken hearts and dreams.

The music, along with candles on each table, evoked a romantic aura. Red-paneled walls, strategically placed track lights and African prints depicting tribal warriors and wildlife provided an atmosphere quite unlike the popular disco clubs frequented by a younger crowd. Sutton's was a place to dine, drink and enjoy the novelty of live music.

The band took a break to eat when the hostesses began serving the advertised entrée. Nicholas sampled the spareribs, greens and rice. He crooked a long finger and she leaned over to hear what he wanted to say.

"How does it measure up against Randy's Rib Rack?"

Dyana bit into a small piece of the succulent meat. "Good," she said. "But not good enough," she concluded.

Bracing an elbow on the table, Nicholas supported his chin on the back of a hand. "One of these weekends we're going to take a ride to Philadelphia where I can stuff myself on your father's ribs, basted with his special *secret* sauce."

"How can I thank you for a most enjoyable evening?" she asked, tilting her head to look up at him.

Nicholas anchored both hands over her head, making no attempt to touch or kiss her. The deep green of her dress made his eyes darker. His chest rose and fell heavily under the black shirt and she felt him shudder as he struggled to control the whorling static rising between them.

One hand gripped her key while the other went to the middle of his chest, feeling the heat of his bare flesh through the silken fabric. Her fingers clutched the shirt in a motion of desperation; she had to hold him and feel as if he were a part of her existence.

Nicholas, closing his eyes, threw back his head and groaned as if in pain. "Dyana!"

Her name, torn from his throat, echoed her longings and she breathed out her own soft whimper. Her fingers tightened in a fist, imprisoning the black silk. His hands slid down to clasp her waist, holding her captive to his surging passions. She did not want to escape when she saw his green eyes open and widen when he read the message in her brown ones, filled with promises of things he'd forgotten. They were brimming with trust, not fear or shadows from her past.

His head came down slowly and deliberately until their moist breaths mingled. His mouth covered hers with complete possession. Silently, wordlessly, he demanded and she gave; willingly and unselfishly. His kiss was greedy in its exploration and she matched it with fire and total surrender.

It ended, both of them gasping for air. One large hand cradled the back of her head, bringing her cheek to his shoulder.

He held her a long time, neither speaking. He shifted, pressing his lips to her forehead.

"Good night, sweetheart."

Pulling out of his loose embrace, she turned away. "Good night." She slipped the key in the lock and pushed open the door.

She would not turn around to look at him again. His footsteps were silent on the carpeted hallway before a soft click of the closing door indicated he was gone. Her eyes were swimming with unshed tears and she knew she had to stop dating Nicholas. Not only had she fallen in love with him, but it was becoming more difficult to see him leave after each date. She was unable to suppress the fear that one day he would walk away and she would never see him again.

"One more day of picking at your food and I'm going to ship you back to Philadelphia where Jesse can worry himself sick over you."

Dyana pulled the blanket up to her shoulders, turning her face into the pillows. "I'm eating."

Susie threw up her hands in a helpless gesture. "You talk to her, Olivia," she pleaded and stalked out of the room.

The mattress gave slightly under Livvy's weight. She put an arm over Dyana's shoulders. "What's wrong, girlfriend?"

Dyana shook her head, biting down on her lower lip. "Nothing. My aunt is overreacting."

Livvy's hand made comforting circular motions on her back. "For once I must agree with your aunt, Dyana. You've been going around with your face dragging the ground for more than a week. What can be so awful that you can't talk to me about it? I'm here for you, friend."

Dyana reached under the pillow for a tissue, wiping her eyes. Nicholas was the problem. He'd canceled their date on Sunday, saying Paul wanted him to represent *Pinnacle* at a convention of magazine publishers in San Francisco. The conference was to last three days, but Nicholas extended it to five.

She managed to complete her research and interview the manager of Apollo Theatre in his absence. After two drafts, she finalized what she felt would be acceptable to the publisher and editor. Even her aunt had praised what she'd written, saying she had captured the mood of the audience when they sat silent, awestruck by the raw talent of a performer on Amateur Night. Not even Susan Randolph's words of encouragement were enough.

She smiled up through her tears at Livvy. "If I tell you, promise me you won't laugh."

"I promise."

"You won't tell my aunt."

Livvy took her hand. "I promise, Dyana."

"And please don't tell Nicholas."

Livvy leaned closer, squinting. "Are you in some kind of trouble?"

"Trouble?" she repeated, dabbing at her swollen eyes.

"Yes, trouble. You know what I mean, Dyana."

"You . . . you think I'm in *that* kind of trouble?" Livvy's head bobbed up and down and Dyana began to laugh while her neighbor stared at her as if she'd taken leave of her senses. "Forget that kind of trouble, Livvy," she sputtered. "The man won't even touch me when he kisses."

"How in the world does he manage to accomplish that feat?"

Dyana continued to smile. "Never mind, he does." She chewed her lower lip again, looking away. "I'm in love with Nicholas Bradshaw," she confessed.

Livvy looked at the pained expression on Dyana's face. Never had she seen her look so defeated. To her, Dyana was invincible; the unsinkable Molly Brown. "What's so wrong with that?"

"It is wrong, Livvy. Not for someone else, but for me." Her voice broke. "I'm twenty-eight years old and I'm no smarter than I was when I was twenty-two." The tears she'd tried holding back fell.

Livvy sighed heavily, wrapping both arms around Dyana's shoulders to hold her until the sobs became soft hiccuping sounds. "Tell me about it, Dee," she urged.

She told her everything, leaving nothing out. "It's like looking at a videotape of my life. I knew Steven for a month before I fell in love with him, and with Nicholas it only took three weeks."

"You were good, girlfriend," Livvy reassured her. "The man would've had me the first day. You were so afraid of giving in to your emotions that you were unable to see what your aunt and I saw the first day he came here to see you. His gentleness was unbelievable. Now you're shocked when you discover the wonder of loving a man," she said in a comforting professional tone. She picked up a tissue and blotted Dyana's moist cheeks. "But you have to remember one thing, Dyana. Nicholas is not Steven. You saw Steven as someone to help you escape from your overprotective parents. In this you failed to see him as someone you could truly love. He became a rescuer, not a friend or even a lover. He certainly could not have become a husband from what you tell me because he only would've been a substitute for your father. And while you were willing to marry him, not once did you think you were trading one form of bondage for another."

Dyana closed her eyes, digesting Livvy's words. "Are you saying I didn't love Steven?"

Livvy was now Dr. Patterson. "You couldn't love him, Dyana. You were afraid of him; afraid of making him angry and constantly seeking his approval for everything. You were willing to overlook his infidelity because you thought you would lose him."

"I did lose him, Livvy."

"Wrong. He lost you. He lost the best woman he probably ever had or will have. Now, take Nicholas Bradshaw."

"What about him?" She ran her hand over her forehead. Her head ached and her eyes felt like rocks behind her skull.

Livvy smiled. "He won't be so easy to shake. The man's as tenacious as a pit bull; he won't give up."

She conjured up Nicholas's face and dissolved into another crying session. If this was love, it was misery. She'd shed more tears the past few days than she had in years. "I can't love him because I'll lose him too."

"I doubt that. What are you going to do when you see him Monday? Run in the opposite direction?"

"I don't know," she groaned.

There were three rapid raps on the door. Susie scurried in, shocking Dyana and Livvy with this rare show of nerves.

"Nicholas is here for you, Dee."

"I don't want to see him," Dyana shouted from under the blanket she had pulled over her head.

"It's too late," Livvy hissed when she spied the tall figure entering the bedroom.

Livvy glanced at Susie and both of them looked at the mound under the blanket. On cue, they left the bedroom to leave Nicholas grinning at the moving form on the bed.

"How long do you intend to hide under that blanket?"

The heat in her body had nothing to do with the blanket when she heard the familiar velvet-soft voice. "Go away. Please. I'm not well."

Nicholas moved over to stand next to the bed. "What's wrong, darling?"

Her temperature went up another degree with the *darling*. "I . . . I don't know. I guess I've come down with some kind of virus."

"Have you seen a doctor?"

"No," came her muffled reply.

"Then how do you know what you have?"

"I just don't feel well, that's all." Why wouldn't he go away and leave her alone?

"Dyana." He leaned over to touch a shoulder. "I've been away for a week and this is how you greet me? What am I to think?"

"Don't think, Nicholas. Go away."

She screamed when the blanket was stripped from her half-clothed body. She scrambled to pull the nightgown down over bare thighs. Pulling her knees up to her chest, she buried her face in the pillow. Before she could inhale to scream again, her face was pressed against a solid shoulder.

Nicholas smoothed back her mussed hair with his fingers and peered down at her face. His breathing stopped. She did look sick. A worried gaze swept over swollen eyes and skin on a nose cracked from incessant blowing. Even her cheeks were gaunt from a loss of weight she could ill afford.

"Don't look at me like that," she said, humiliated that he saw her looking like a hag. He, on the other hand, had never looked better. The California sun had tanned him to a rich dark golden brown and his hair had grown out to where it curled around his ears.

"Why not?" He was unsuccessful when he couldn't conceal a smile.

"Because I look like a witch."

He lowered his head to kiss her mouth. "Then I guess I'll have to become a warlock, won't I?"

One slender hand pressed against his chest. "Don't kiss me, Nicholas," she pleaded.

"Why? Because I might catch what you have, sweetheart?" Thick, black arching eyebrows lifted when she lowered her gaze. He buried his face in her hair. "Are you afraid I might catch a sickness called love?"

Her head jerked up. A violent trembling shook her and she pressed the back of her hand to her lips. "No."

"Are you afraid I might love you as much as you love me?"

Tears filled her eyes, but didn't fall. "Who told you?"

Nicholas kissed her eyelids, gathering her tightly to his chest. "You did," he replied confidently. "You did each time you smiled and laughed; each time I kissed you and you lowered those barriers where I was able to know the real Dyana Randolph. You don't know how much I wanted to touch you and communicate what I was feeling, darling."

Her fingers traced his cheek to move down to the cleft in his chin. "I don't understand it. I thought I was someone you wanted to amuse yourself with. After all I'm neither a model . . ."

"Don't," he warned, placing a finger over her lips. "I only went out with them because my publicist thought it would enhance my image. He claimed it helped to sell books."

"Did it?" She snuggled against his muscular warmth.

The laughter began deep in his chest and bubbled upward. "I hope not. It would be crushing to my literary ego if it did. I'd take some empty-headed chit out a few times, get our photo in a paper or magazine, then we'd go our separate ways. The so-called torrid affairs were nothing more than a gimmick and a boost for both of our careers." His hands tightened on her waist. "Now, take you."

"What about me?" she mumbled dreamlike against his chest.

"You're different, Dyana. You're not the kind of woman I can mess over."

Her body went rigid and she pulled out of his arms. "What do you mean by that?"

Nicholas slipped a long brown finger under the narrow strap of her nightgown to pull it up over her shoulder. His full mouth curved into a devastating smile. "What I'm saying, Miss Randolph, is that you're the type of woman a man commits himself to and marries."

Her mouth dropped, then snapped shut. "No, Nicholas."

"Yes, Dyana. I said it and I meant it." His hands went to her shoulders to shake her gently. "No more hiding. Open your eyes," he ordered when she closed them against his intense glare. "You're good for me and I'm good for you and I don't intend to spend the rest of my life chasing you."

His overconfident tone irked her. "You give yourself too much importance."

"Because I tell you that I love you?" he questioned incredulously.

Her small fist struck his chest and he looked down in surprise. "No. Because you think I'm going to fall at your feet because you're Nicholas Bradshaw!"

"I'm not asking you to fall at my feet, darling," he explained. "I'm only asking you to marry me."

She stared, not blinking as he ran a forefinger down the length of her tender nose to her parted lips. His mouth replaced his finger.

"Say yes!" came Livvy's and Susie's voices in unison outside of the closed door.

Dyana gasped, horrified that her aunt and friend had overheard everything.

"I'll try to be a good husband to you," Nicholas continued in a lower tone which could not be overheard by the eavesdropping pair outside of the door. "I have my moods, but normally I'm rather easygoing. I eat everything except brussels sprouts and liver. I have a full-time housekeeper which will leave you more time for your career. If you don't like the house, you can choose something more to your liking. I want children," he rushed on, "but I'm willing to wait if that's what you want."

She wanted to laugh, but didn't when she saw a flash of uncertainty in his eyes. Nicholas Bradshaw was trying to sell himself to her because he was afraid she would reject his proposal. She touched his cheek, registering the tension. She loved him; she loved him with everything she had and she knew then that she had never been in love before. Both arms circled his strong neck as she leaned into his strength.

"Now, tell me why you really want to marry me," she mumbled against his throat.

His fingers became tentacles on her waist. They ceased to exist as separate entities, becoming one in love and spirit.

"If it means that I want to wake up with you by my side each morning, and come home to you and not an empty house, and if I can watch your belly swell with our children while I spend the rest of my life telling you that I love you, then, Dyana Randolph, I want you as my wife and partner."

He was offering her all that she'd hoped for. It was a chance to share her dreams and her future with him.

"Yes," she breathed out. The single spoken word conveyed all that she felt for the man holding her to his heart.

Nicholas set her away from him, bringing a finger to his lips to motion her not to speak. His jogging shoes were silent when he crept across the room. Dyana clapped both hands over her mouth to keep from laughing when he pulled open the door and Livvy and Susie fell to the floor.

His face was solemn when he helped Susie regain her balance. "She turned me down," he stated.

"What!" Susie cried.

"No," moaned Livvy.

Susie pulled her apron to her face to hide the tears and Dyana was shocked at her aunt's reaction.

"Don't believe him!" she shouted. "He's only paying you back for snooping. We *are* going to be married."

Livvy squealed and threw her arms around Susie. Dyana

looked at Nicholas and smiled. He returned her smile and she was filled with a sense of fulfillment for the first time in her life. She'd been allowed a second chance.

"When is the big day?" Michael asked across the table.

"Six weeks," Susie answered for her niece.

"Why the rush?"

Susie frowned at Michael, but didn't say anything. If it had been up to her, Dyana and Nicholas would've eloped the night before.

Dyana peered up at Michael through her lashes. "We see no point in having a long engagement."

"Perhaps you've got that right," Michael mused. "Make certain I get an invitation, that's all."

"Why shouldn't you? Just because you're no longer with the magazine doesn't mean I don't know where you live, Mr. Dalton."

He pulled at the hair over his ear and turned his sad gaze on her beaming face. "I plan to do some moving around now that I have the time, and I don't want to be out of the country when your big day arrives."

"Where are you going, Michael?" Susie asked.

"I'm going to Mobile to visit my daughter and her kids for a few weeks, then maybe I'll take a cruise to the Caribbean."

"Globetrot all you want, Michael Dalton, but you'd better be back in time for my wedding."

"Yes, ma'am."

Her joy knew no bounds when she called her parents to tell them that she was to be married. Edna Randolph began to cry and Jesse Randolph had to take the receiver from his wife's trembling hand.

"What do you want me to prepare, princess?"

"Please, Daddy. Nothing fancy or too big. It's going to be for family and close friends, not the local high school."

"Don't tell me . . ."

"I'll elope," she threatened.

There came a choking sound. "Anything you want, princess," Jesse conceded. "I don't want you to cheat me out of the honor of walking you down the aisle to give you away, baby. You don't know how I felt when your brothers got married and I saw my daughters-in-law walk down the aisle looking so very lovely on their fathers' arms. All I could think of was the day I would do the same with my princess."

"And you will have the honor, Daddy," she whispered. She still found it difficult to believe how much her father had mellowed. Her moving away had changed him. It had changed the both of them.

"And you tell this Bradshaw fellow that he'd better be good to you or he'll have to answer to the Randies. All of them!"

She laughed. The four Randolph brothers' reputation was well known in North Philly when they were growing up. Teenage boys had acquired excellent peripheral vision whenever she walked down the streets. None of them wanted to be accused of trying to *hit on* the sister of the Randies.

Monday morning found Dyana affecting a pace she'd never experienced before. Her feet never seemed to touch the ground. Nicholas ushered her into his office as soon as she arrived, closing the door.

"I have to go to Washington," he informed her as soon as she'd recovered from his hungry, possessive kiss.

Her fingers touched her throbbing mouth. "Why, Nicholas?"

His fingers curved around her upper arms. "Ronnie Murphy called this morning to report Carl may be released from prison. Apparently her attorney has uncovered some evidence which may prove her husband's innocence. I'm afraid it might also uncover a conspiracy within the past administration," he explained in a terse tone.

She flinched when she recognized the tension in his voice. "Will any of this affect the future of Carl's book?"

Nicholas picked up a garment bag and leather tote from a chair. "I don't believe it should," he replied. "I've got to leave now if I'm going to make a ten-thirty shuttle." His eyes searched her face quickly before looking away. "I don't know how long I'll be in Washington, Dyana. If you need me for any reason, call. I've left the Murphys' address and number on your desk."

She nodded, feeling the loss before his leaving. Except for the few hours on Saturday, she had not spent any time with him for more than a week. "I'm going to miss you, Nicholas."

He offered a nod, his expression impassive. And without saying anything else, he walked out of the office.

She stood in the same spot for a long time, her arms clasped tightly around her body. There was no good-bye kiss or embrace or any indication he would miss her. She began to wonder if her willingness to become his wife had dampened his urgency for pursuit and possession. Had the thrill gone out of the chase now that he knew she would be his?

EIGHT

Dyana compensated for Nicholas's absence by immersing herself in her project. She entered the mailing list into the computer and composed a form letter, making inquiries as to new exhibits, musical openings, areas of restoration, state festivals and unusual local personalities. She arrived early, worked late and called to have her lunch delivered.

She swore Inez to secrecy, telling her she wanted to wait for Nicholas's return to make the announcement official. Inez promptly closed the office door and let out a blood-curdling scream, having to explain with a sheepish look on her face to the other employees that she thought she saw a mouse. The building's exterminator acted by sending a man to check for the nonexistent rodent.

Dyana smiled at Livvy's reflection in the full-length mirror as Susie basted the pure iris-blue chiffon on her frame.

"Do you like this color?" Livvy asked.

"Stop wiggling," Susie ordered as she slipped pins along the length.

Dyana pulled up her legs, tucking her bare feet under her body. "The dress and color are perfect for you, Livvy," she reassured her maid of honor.

The dress was a trailing wisp of airy fabric with a short sleeve of ruffles cascading along the side of a blouson bodice and falling down the back to the hem of the floor-length dress.

Livvy twisted to get a better view of the back. "Of course I'll wear my contact lenses because these red frames will be hideous with this color blue."

"Quit wiggling, Olivia. A few pinholes will make you stiff in a hurry," Susie warned.

Dyana picked up a small hat in blue, festooned with tiny violets on streamers of ribbon. She gazed absentmindedly at her own dress hanging over the dress form. There was no need to alter it because Susie had made it to fit her dimensions; it was the ivory organza she had designed on a whim.

"Have you heard from Nicholas, Dyana?" Livvy asked.

"No."

"Mind your business, Olivia." Susie was back to her former relationship with her neighbor. "He's a busy man and if he had the time he would've called."

"I only asked," Livvy retorted.

"Then don't," snapped Susie. "Knowing you, you'd probably want to go on their honeymoon with them."

"We won't get a chance to take a honeymoon until the end of the year," Dyana informed them.

"Why not?" Susie asked. "I thought the two of you were going to take a few days off."

"Even that is off." She twisted a stray strand of hair around her forefinger. "Nicholas has been away a great deal, and there are too many changes taking place for him to be away again until the end of the year."

"All you'll have is a Saturday night and Sunday together before you return to work?"

"Don't fret, Livvy. Nicholas and I will then have a very special Christmas to share with one another. Not only will it be our first Christmas together, but also a belated honeymoon."

The ringing of the telephone penetrated her sleep and Dyana lay in the darkness for several seconds before reaching over for the receiver.

"Hello," she mumbled sleepily.

"Dee, it's me," came a male voice.

She sat up quickly. "Evan?" she asked, her heart racing in trepidation. Why was her brother calling her? "What time is it?" Now she was fully awake.

"It's almost two. I didn't want to call at this hour, but Mom wanted me to."

There was a click. "What's the matter?" Susie asked on the extension.

"There's been a fire and explosion in the store and Dad didn't take the news too well. He collapsed and the doctor has suggested he spend a few days in the hospital to undergo some tests . . ."

"Be at the station to pick us up on the first train," she shouted at her brother, hanging up.

It finally sank in when Susie walked into the bedroom, her face streaked with tears. She ran toward her aunt, throwing her arms around her.

"He's going to be all right, Auntie. Daddy's tough. He's going to make it," she said, trying to reassure Susie as well as herself.

She had come home. The pleasant smells coming from the large country kitchen in Paoli brought back a wealth of good and bad memories. Dyana watched her mother's slight figure as she bustled around the kitchen.

"I don't know how I've put up with that man for these past thirty-five years," Edna Randolph continued to grumble. "I told him to cut out smoking those smelly old cigars, but would he listen to me? Oh no. He had to wait to give his good hard-earned money to a doctor before he decides to throw away those weeds. I'd say to him, 'Jesse, those things are going to be the death of you yet.' He'd cough and wheeze and continue puffing like a chimney. Then when he suffers a shock his body's not strong enough to bounce back."

She stopped complaining long enough to note the amused look on her daughter's face. "I hope the man you intend to marry turns out to be as stubborn as your father so you'll know what I've had to put up with all of these years."

"I'm not laughing at you Mom. It's just that I've heard the same thing for as long as I can remember and nothing has changed. Daddy's home and resting and you should be grateful for that."

Edna ceased stirring the gravy in a large pot, giving her daughter a frown. "Your father's elevated blood pressure will prove to be a lot less damaging than his depression over losing the store. The time and money he's poured into that business represents his life, Dee. The proceeds have allowed us to buy this house and educate five children. After we retire or are no longer alive, the money will be for our children and grandchildren."

She was going to apologize for not realizing her mother's position when the doorbell rang.

"I'll get it," shouted Evan from somewhere in the house.

"I hope that's not Mrs. Mitchell nagging me about her daughter's sweet sixteen party. I told her we would provide the food even though we don't have the store. There's nothing wrong with Edna Randolph's kitchen. After all, Jesse began in a kitchen."

Evan stuck his head in the kitchen. He was still wearing the sweat suit he used for jogging. "You have company, Dee," he said, pulling off his shirt. "Wait dinner for me, Mom."

"Don't rush," Edna called out to her youngest son. "We still have to wait for Tom and Walt."

Dyana pulled an old paint-spattered shirt of Evan's over a tank top. She and Susie had been in Paoli, a suburb of Philadelphia, for two days. Jesse Randolph was kept overnight in Philadelphia General for tests and released to a house filled with his children and twin sister. He was embarrassed by all of the attention and retreated behind the door of his bedroom to escape.

She walked into the living room and saw him. She missed the weariness lining his face when she flung herself against him.

"Nicky!"

Gathering her tightly, Nicholas's hands swept over her back. He picked her up, swinging her around. "Hi, kitten."

"Hi, yourself," she whispered. She tightened her grip on his neck, never wanting to be apart from him again.

He set her on her feet, cradling her face between his

hands. "I missed you, love," he confessed. "I've missed you so much," he moaned, placing tiny kisses on her moist, parted mouth.

"Why didn't you call me?" she asked between the soft, nibbling kisses.

Nicholas pressed her to his chest, her cheek resting against his shoulder. "I didn't call you because I was afraid that if I'd heard your voice I wouldn't have stayed to complete what I had to do. Three hundred miles away and you still haunt me."

"How did you know where to find me?"

He pulled back to give her a tired smile. "I called your place and when I didn't get an answer I called Livvy. She told me about the fire and gave me your parents' address. That phone call saved me from flying into New York only to have to turn around and catch another plane to Philadelphia."

A car's horn blared loudly in the stillness of the late afternoon. "I have to pay the driver and get my bags," he said. He pushed open the screen door to return to the taxi.

"Dee, who are you entertaining on the porch?"

Dyana placed a finger over her lips and motioned to her mother. "Come and get a sneak preview of what you're going to have for a son-in-law."

Edna quickened her steps and peered over her daughter's shoulder through the mesh of the door. She cocked her head to one side. Small, slanting eyes in a cinnamon-brown face narrowed appreciably.

"Now what will Hattie McGee say when she sees what my daughter has brought home? Catty old mealy-mouth gossip. She's always shootin' her mouth off about the man her Charlene married. He only married her because no one else wanted him. I'm going to have her come over after the wedding just to give her an eyeful."

"Don't you dare," Dyana whispered in horror.

"I dare anything," Edna promised.

"Don't tell me you're still feuding with Mrs. McGee after all of these years."

Edna shook her head covered with iron-gray short curls. "I'm not fighting with Hattie," she said in a tone which indicated she had been insulted. "She fights with me."

Dyana hugged her mother. "Isn't thirty-five years long enough for her to realize she can't have Jesse Randolph? She had Daddy but lost him when he married you."

"Hattie never had Jesse."

"That's not what Daddy says," Dyana teased.

Edna sucked her teeth loudly. "Jesse is not known for always telling the truth where it concerns him and Hattie. To tell you the truth, Hattie *was* the reason I wanted out of Philadelphia. After her Willie died she used to come into the store battin' her moon-looking eyes at my husband. But I fooled her; she didn't count on my working at the store everyday and stopped coming in. Living here in Paoli was a little too far for her to just drop in and with me in the store she didn't want to take any chances that I might see her flirting with my Jesse."

Dyana dropped a kiss on her mother's cheek. "You were jealous of Daddy?"

Edna watched Nicholas as he walked up the path and up the stairs to the porch. "Wouldn't you be of your husband?"

Dyana's face brightened with a captivating smile. "Yes. I'm sure I would," she added.

Edna held the door open for Nicholas. "Please come in and rest yourself. As soon as Dyana gets you settled, we'll see about getting some food into you."

Nicholas dropped his tote and garment bag, leaning down to kiss his future mother-in-law's cheek. "Thanks for the invitation." Raising his head, he sniffed the air like a large cat. "Do I smell roast turkey?"

Edna's face split with a wide grin. "Why yes, Mr. Bradshaw."

"Nicholas," he insisted.

Edna folded her hands on a pair of narrow hips most would not have believed carried five babies, four of them weighing more than nine pounds. "If it's going to be Nicholas, then you must call me Edna. Only people I don't care for have to address me as Mrs. Randolph."

If Dyana was surprised with the interchange between her mother and fiancé she did not reveal it. Edna Randolph did not take readily to most people and her apparent openness was a rare display of affection. It had taken a long time before she and Susie were able to offer each other a civil word without an argument. Dyana's decision to move in with her aunt forced the sisters-in-law to communicate with each other as members of the same family for the first time in twenty years.

Evan walked into the living room, freshly groomed from his shower. He smiled at Nicholas. "Sorry about running off like I did. A couple of miles of jogging hadn't prepared me for greeting company." He extended a hand. "Evan."

Nicholas shook his hand. "Nicholas Bradshaw."

"Hey, you're the man who's going to marry my sister," he said when he registered who Nicholas was.

Dyana saw Nicholas tense. Had he anticipated some opposition?

"You're right about that."

Evan pumped his hand harder. "Well, all right. Welcome to the family." He threw his arms around his back, thumping it loudly.

"Thanks, Dr. Randolph."

Evan looked to the floor. "Another year of medical school, internship and a residency. Then you'll be able to call me doctor."

Nicholas dropped an arm around the younger man's shoulders. "It's going to be a while before you get used to the title. I can't see any harm in practicing. Do you?"

"Can't do any harm," Evan agreed. He picked up Nicholas's luggage. "Come on, brother. Let's get you settled in before the rest of the family invades us. You'll get to meet everyone except for my oldest brother Jesse. He's in Africa saving souls." He stared at Nicholas staring back at his sister. "Hey, fella, she's not going anywhere," he laughed over his shoulder when he led the way up the stairs to the bedrooms.

There were Randolphs in varying heights and looks around the large dining room table. Dyana sat between Nicholas and Evan, facing Susie. Edna and Susie had outdone themselves and a golden turkey with a sausage-cornbread dressing, giblet gravy, smothered cabbage, potato salad and bread pudding with a brandy sauce were set out on the table. The wives of Thomas and Walter divided their time between the dining room and the kitchen to supervise their children who had begun arguing over which current rock star was better.

"See what you have to look forward to, Nicholas?" Tom said.

Nicholas glanced up from his plate, seemingly upset that he'd been interrupted from finishing his meal. "It sounds interesting," he stated solemnly.

"It's instant insanity," Evan remarked, grinning at his sister. His clear brown eyes sparkled with a mischievous gleam. "I'm willing to wager Dyana has the twins. What do you think, Walt?"

Walter, resembling his mother more than any other of the Randolph offspring, nodded. "How much, Ev? Put up or shut up."

"Twenty dollars."

"Can't you do better than that, little brother?"

"Don't forget that I'm still a student, big brother. Twenty dollars is big bucks to me."

"You're on," Walt agreed.

Nicholas, following the friendly interchange, laughed. "I would've staked you if you needed a bigger bankroll, Evan. You'll probably win because twins are prevalent in my family. *Every* generation."

Walt groaned loudly and Evan reached over Dyana's head to give Nicholas an exaggerated high-five. Their theatrics set the stage for a meal filled with laughter and jokes as the elder Randolph remained in bed, resting comfortably under the effects of the sedative the doctor had prescribed.

Nicholas patted his flat midsection over the red tee shirt.

"My compliments to the chefs," he announced, bowing to Edna and Susie. "How does one not get fat around this place?"

Evan flexed narrow shoulders under his own polo. "It helps to have a high metabolic rate as well as a regular regimen of exercise. It's a good thing I'm not home all year or I would give Dad a little competition."

"Daddy doesn't eat very much when he sits down at the table," Dyana informed Nicholas. "However, he does sample his dishes, shall we say, quite frequently."

Nicholas held out his cup for another serving of a fragrant blend of almond mocha creme coffee. "I'm waiting to sample those ribs I've heard so much about."

"You'll have to wait for my father for that," Tom said.

"No you won't," Edna announced.

All eyes were fixed on Edna's smug, smiling face. "Jesse gave me the recipe."

"When?" came a loud chorus of voices from around the table.

"When the old coot thought he was going to die, that's when," Edna said with a frown. "He was lying in the hospital mumbling the ingredients when I thought he was praying to save his sinful hide. I was so mad I wanted to choke him."

Susie began laughing and soon everyone joined in, pounding the table and wiping away the tears streaming down their faces.

Dyana sat on the wicker rocker, reveling in the warm air brushing her face. Nicholas sat less than a foot away, staring out at the blackness of the night.

"You have a wonderful family, Dyana, and I'm glad that I can think of them as my family."

She smiled. "They're all right; a little crazy, but all right."

"They're warm and wonderful. Just like you, sweetheart."

She moved closer and pulled up her legs to support her back against his shoulder. "When will I get to meet your parents and sister?"

One arm tightened on her shoulder. "Probably not until

the wedding. My parents live in Hawaii but they'll fly in a week before to stay with my sister who lives in Louisiana. I've notified my mother's brother and his wife who'll come in from Chicago."

"They seem to be spread out all over the country."

"We Bradshaws are a wandering lot. We probably are descendants of a nomadic tribe from the Sahara." He stood up, pulling her with him. "Let's go for a walk."

"You're mad!" she hissed. "It's after midnight."

"I know what time it is. I can't neck out here on the porch with your family less than fifty feet away."

"You are crazy!"

"I know, Miss Randolph. I'm crazy about you."

They didn't neck. They were content to walk along the road holding hands. There was a strange silence between them and neither felt the need to initiate conversation.

The sound of gravel on an unpaved portion of the road grated loudly under their feet when they retraced their steps. A half moon hung suspended in the star-littered sky, providing a measure of illumination as Dyana led the way over the familiar path. This homecoming would be remembered as the most important aside from when she would return to become the wife of the man beside her.

She stood on the top step, smiling down at him. "Good night, darling."

Nicholas reached up to capture her chin. "Good night, sweetheart." He didn't get a chance to kiss her when she turned quickly to go into the house. He smiled, rocking back on his heels. He waited for several minutes, then followed.

Dyana sat beside her father's bed, holding his hand. "You're going to have to make a few promises and keep them, Daddy."

Jesse Randolph smiled, not opening his eyes. "You sound like your mother, princess. The woman is beginning to haunt me." He opened his eyes to stare up at the face which reminded him of his own mother. "She yells at me, Dee."

"Mom never yells."

"If it's not yelling, it's nagging. She wakes me up to nag me about taking my medication, and she's beginning to nag me about working. Claims I'm working too hard. I've always worked hard. A man never accomplished a thing warmin' up the seat of his pants."

"You've paid your dues, Daddy. It's time to let someone else take over."

A frown settled between eyes which had become less bright with increasing age. "Who? Certainly not Evan. He wants to be a doctor and push pills down someone's throat. Tom's happy teaching school, and Jesse's made his home in Africa."

"You forget about Walt. He's not happy working where he is and he's the one with the business background. Let him take over for you."

Jesse's chest rose and fell slowly. "I'll think about it, princess. I'll think about it," he repeated, slurring.

Dyana kissed her father's whiskered cheek and pulled the sheet up over his chest. The medication was taking effect. She sat watching him, thinking of the times when he would've never listened to her suggestions.

It was a time for change; for everyone. She never would've thought she would trust another man again or accept his proposal of marriage, or even consider making arrangements to walk down the aisle of the same church where she stood sobbing out her heart six years before. She waited until she heard her father's soft snoring, then slipped from the room, closing the door softly.

"Where are you off to in such a rush?"

Dyana pulled a lightweight windbreaker over her blouse. "Nicholas is going to pick me up at the station. If I don't make the nine o'clock train, I'll have to wait an hour for another."

"Call him and tell him you're going to make the next one."

"Susie," she groaned, shoving her keys, wallet and loose change into her shoulder bag.

"Do it, Dyana. It's important."

She froze, turning slowly to stare at her aunt. Susie's tone said everything and revealed nothing. "What's wrong?"

Susie had not begun dressing for church and that should've been a clue that all was not right this Sunday morning.

"Call Nicholas," she ordered.

Dyana picked up the telephone and dialed. She counted off the rings until she heard the break in the connection.

"Nicholas Bradshaw."

"Nicholas, this is Dyana."

"Good morning darling. I . . ."

"I'm going to be late," she interrupted. "I'm taking a later train."

"Is something wrong?"

She heard the concern in the deep voice but at this point she knew no more than he did. "I don't know. I'll be there on the next train."

Dyana had planned to spend the day at Nicholas's house rearranging most of her clothes and books which had been shipped the week before. Her bedroom in her aunt's brownstone building held only what she would need for the next week. In less than seven days she would no longer come home to the building on Convent Avenue. In only seven days she would become Dyana Bradshaw and go home with her husband each night.

"Michael!" she cried out when she entered the kitchen. She threw her arm around his neck and kissed him loudly on his cheek. "When did you get back?"

He patted her head. "Last night. I told you I wouldn't miss my best girl's wedding."

"How was Mobile and your grandchildren?"

"Mobile was too hot and my grandchildren got on my nerves. They forget their grandpa has slowed down. All they wanted to eat was fast food. I'm beginning to feel like a Whopper Mac and thick shake."

"It's either a Whopper or Big Mac, Michael," Susie said, correcting him gently.

"Thank you, Susan. Whatever the heck it is, I missed your food." He stared at Susie, communicating a secret message.

Susie glanced up at a kettle-shaped clock over the sink. "I've got to talk with Dee. She has to leave to make a train."

Michael settled back in the chair, tugging at his hair. "I'm in no hurry, Susan."

Dyana listened, shocked, as Susie revealed the latest news about Jesse Randolph's business future.

"I can't believe the insurance company won't cover all of the damages," she almost cried. "Where will Daddy get that much money?"

"I don't know," Susie whispered through her fingers. "He's talking about taking out a mortgage on the house."

"He can't do that," Dyana said. "He's too old to start worrying about paying off another mortgage."

Susie lowered her hands. "I have some money saved, but most of my equity is in this brownstone building. Maybe I'll sell it."

"And live where?" Dyana asked.

"Ladies! Please!" Michael roared. He held up his hand. "Selling homes and refinancing mortgages are all wrong."

"You tell us what is right, Michael Dalton," Susie challenged. Her golden eyes were snapping with fire.

"Your brother, and your father," he said acknowledging each woman, "needs an investor. Someone who is willing to invest money in his business."

"My father happens to run a small store, not a Burger King franchise."

"But he could establish a franchise with the right backers," Michael insisted.

"I don't think Donald Trump is interested in spareribs, Michael."

Michael glared at Susie, ignoring her sharp retort. "But I am. I have more money than I could ever hope to spend, and I don't need relatives standing around like ravenous wolves waiting for me to kick off so they can fight over it."

Dyana leaned forward. "What are you saying?"

"What I am saying is that I'm willing to loan your father

the money he needs to complete the necessary repairs, but on one condition."

"What?" Dyana and Susie asked in unison.

"That he set up another store in a different location. From what I've heard the man has the Midas touch. He can hire someone to manage the second site or divide his time between the two."

"Daddy is in no shape to manage one site full time and you're asking him to take on two?"

"There is a thing called employees and managers, Dyana," he retorted with a saccharine grin. He glanced up at the clock. "You'd better get going if you're going to make that train. Susan and I will talk this out and let you know what we've decided to do. Go," he insisted when she didn't move.

"Are you sure?"

"Don't worry, Dee. Michael and I will work something out."

Dyana spent the time riding the subway and then the Metro-North thinking about her father. She didn't want to believe everything he'd worked for could go up in a puff of smoke. An inadequately installed hot water heater had been the source of the explosion and fire and the fire marshal had reported this finding to the insurance investigator. The insurance company had denied 90 percent of the claim, leaving Jesse Randolph to seek outside sources to recover his losses. All of the plans for her wedding were overshadowed when she considered her family's plight. How could she be so deliriously happy when her parents' future loomed so bleakly?

NINE

Dyana sat beside her mother, holding her tightly. The time was drawing closer when she would take her vows and become Mrs. Nicholas Bradshaw and she still was unable to still the attack of nerves threatening to overcome her normally unflappable composure.

"Are all brides this way or is it just me?" she asked her mother tearfully, trembling in spite of the effort it took to steady her quaking limbs.

Edna pulled back to place a cool hand on her daughter's forehead. A slight frown marred her smooth brow when she saw the fright mirrored in the large brown eyes beneath thick, long lashes. "You're quite calm compared to the way I was," she informed her, hoping to instill a measure of confidence in the younger woman. "After it's all over you'll wonder just what it was you had to be so nervous about."

Edna went over to an open closet door and touched the froth of whiteness suspended on a hanger. "Susie has outdone herself with this dress." She smiled. "It's been a time for miracles. You're getting married and Jesse has been given a chance to resurrect his business with your friend's loan."

"How long did he and Daddy argue about how they wanted things done?"

"Believe it or not, they didn't argue. Michael had everything spelled out on paper and Jesse had Walt look it over. Walt gave his approval and your father signed his name. Walt also agreed to quit his job at the bank and take over. The three of them were talking about packaging Jesse's sauce for mass distribution."

"Because you know the recipe he feels the world should also know it?"

Edna shot her daughter a wistful look, admiring the shiny red streaks in the dark brown hair. "If I live to be a hundred, I'll never understand what makes a man what he is."

Dyana laughed, expelling some of her apprehension and settled back on the mound of pillows to relax. She had tried taking a nap, but that proved unsuccessful. The murmur of voices had floated up from the lower floor and she tried distinguishing one from the other.

Susie had become her confidante when at different intervals she reported who had arrived. Nicholas's parents, aunt and uncle and his sister and her husband had arrived the night before, staying over in a hotel in Philadelphia. The Randolphs had opened their home for a brunch for the out-of-town guests, setting the mood for the festivities to occur later that afternoon.

She was still propped up on the pile of pillows when Livvy slipped quietly into the room an hour later. Without her glasses she appeared younger, with a wide-eyed look of innocence.

"Why aren't you dressed, girlfriend?" she admonished, shaking a forefinger

Dyana sat up, smiling at her maid of honor. "How beautiful you look, Livvy." Her best friend and now ex-neighbor was stunning in the delicate blue chiffon dress with the small hat perched jauntily on her head. Only a wisp of curls was revealed along her neckline. Several streamers hung from the hat down her back.

Livvy sat on the bed, spreading out the dress to avoid wrinkling it. "Are you ready for your big day?"

Dyana swung her legs over the bed. She fluffed up her coiffed hair to where it was full and bouncy above her shoulders. "The day is perfect. The sun is shining and all of my loved ones are here to help me celebrate one of the most important days of my life, and I'm so in love with Nicholas that I'm scared to death."

"If it's any consolation, girlfriend, the man looks as if he's going to pass out. I never thought he would be so uptight. Anyone that speaks to him has to repeat what they say at least twice before he's able to respond," Livvy informed her like a coconspirator. "Your brothers haven't been too cooperative. They tease him every chance they get."

"Maybe he's getting cold feet, Livvy."

"I don't believe that," Livvy replied, reaching up to help her out of the robe. "He keeps asking Evan if he has the ring and manages to check his watch every ten minutes. You should've scheduled the ceremony for the morning instead of the afternoon, girlfriend. It appears as if Nicholas Bradshaw is somewhat impatient to make you his wife."

"I just want this over as much as he does."

The past few weeks had been stressful for Nicholas. The pressures at the magazine had escalated as well as Carl Murphy's tenuous future. His attorney submitted evidence, hoping to appeal the conviction, and Ronnie Murphy called several times a day to keep Nicholas abreast of all of the changes.

The employees of Westgate Publishing, with Livvy and Susie's intervention, had given her a lingerie shower. The tiny scraps of silk, satin and nylon left her cheeks burning long after she replaced each item in a box and left them for Nicholas to take back to his house. He compounded her embarrassment when he dangled a black negligee from a finger saying it wasn't quite his size.

The pace was accelerated when a stack of mail in response to her column was left on her desk one morning. The return address on one envelope piqued her curiosity as she slid the letter opener under the flap to uncover the contents. Her eyes skimmed the single page of typing. She had received a positive inquiry about the collection of American Art from the curator of the Amon Carter Museum in Fort Worth, Texas. Checking with Nicholas for his approval, she called the curator to confirm her trip for the following month.

Livvy finished buttoning the tiny covered buttons along the back of the gown and steered Dyana over to the full-length mirror on the closet door. She adjusted the off-the-shoulder neckline.

"You're a beautiful bride, Dyana," she whispered.

Dyana stared at her reflection. Yards of lace and organza rustled loudly in the silence. She ran her tongue over her lips when Livvy settled the headpiece on her hair. Reaching up with trembling hands, she snatched it off.

"What's the matter, Dyana?"

She closed her eyes, her breath coming quickly. "It's nothing like it was six years ago, but everything is the same. The same bedroom, the same mirror and . . ."

"Stop it! That was your past. Leave it alone," Livvy rasped.

Dyana held out her arms and Livvy pulled her close, offering comfort and support. They held each other until Susie walked into the bedroom to say it was time to leave.

Dyana was certain her father could feel her shaking as she took small, sure steps which would eventually bring her to the side of the man standing at the front of the church waiting to make her his wife.

The shadowy veil concealed the smiling faces of family members and close friends who had come to witness the ceremony joining a Randolph and Bradshaw in the banns of matrimony. As she came closer to Nicholas she discovered the nervousness waning and the joy within her heart swelling until she was certain she would faint from the soaring rapture. A slight smile curved her lips as she continued to focus on the whiteness of the double-breasted jacket, using it as her guide.

The soft strains of the organ playing the wedding march ended. Her father relinquished his claim, stepping back as Nicholas reached out to draw her to his side and the minister asked who was giving her to this man.

She raised her head slightly to glimpse the whiteness of his teeth in a darkly tanned face. She returned the smile, her eyes sweeping quickly over his black shiny hair brushed off his high forehead, the glittering dark green eyes and the sensual curve of his fascinating mouth. His left hand closed gently over her fingers before he turned his attention back to the minister who was waiting to begin the ceremony.

Dyana half-listened to the words; it was as if she were a spectator at play, watching the actors in their roles. Only when she heard Nicholas repeat his vows did she bring her attention back to what was taking place.

"I, Nicholas Reynolds, take thee . . ."

Her lips mouthed his words before she began her own. "I, Dyana Jessica, take thee, Nicholas Reynolds to be my lawfully wedded husband . . ." Was that her voice, low and husky?

The exchange of rings and then it was over. The minister was telling Nicholas he could kiss his wife and she felt her veil being raised. Tears filled her eyes and clung to her lashes as he leaned over to seal his troth.

A wide gold band with yellow and white diamonds on her left hand caught the light from the flickering tapers when her fingers slipped up the front of the tucked shirt. His face swirled in a nebulous haze when he gathered her tightly to his body, increasing the pressure until she thought she was going to faint. Somewhere outside of her head she heard her brother's voice.

"There will be plenty of time for that later tonight, my man," Evan whispered loudly and Livvy giggled behind her bouquet of flowers.

She lowered her head when he released her, keeping her gaze on the length of the red carpet as he led her down the aisle and out of the church.

Dyana vaguely remembered the pop of flashbulbs and a showering with a hail of rice before the wedding party returned to the Randolph house to begin the reception.

Jesse and Edna had opted to open their home instead of utilizing the more formal restaurant or dining hall. Baskets of white flowers in every conceivable variety filled the sun parlor and the living and dining rooms. Large white satin bows graced the highly polished railing of the stairs leading to the second floor level and yards of lace in pristine white graced the many banquet tables set up in each room.

Elaborate ice molds held bottles of wine and champagne while silver serving pieces contained seductive and extravagant dishes ranging from fresh caviar, pâté de foie gras and escargots to garnishes of miniature ears of pickled corn and olives stuffed with hot peppers and anchovies.

The introductions were endless. Cousins and in-laws. She was greeted warmly by Nicholas's parents and his sister and her husband. His mother was a tall, silver-haired woman with dark gray eyes and a dimpled smile.

After the first hour the adults chatted politely with each other while the younger children retreated outdoors to sit on the grass and listen to a popular music station.

Nicholas held a glass of champagne in one hand while the other gripped the fingers of his new wife.

"Did I tell you how lovely you look, Mrs. Bradshaw?"

She blushed. He was the first one to call her by her new name. "Yes. Your eyes tell it all, Mr. Bradshaw."

He was exquisite-looking in his formal dress. A white double-breasted jacket, tucked white shirt with a wing collar, pale pink bow tie, matching cummerbund and pale gray dress slacks set him apart from the other men in the room. He'd confessed that Carl Murphy would've been his best man if Carl had had his freedom, and requested that Evan do the honor.

Michael arrived in time for the ceremony and seemed to attach himself to Susie once everyone returned to the house. Dyana waved to him, blowing a kiss. He returned the kiss and wended his way through the crowd to where she and Nicholas were standing.

He extended his hand to Nicholas. "Congratulations, Nick. It looks as if the best man won the ultimate prize."

Nicholas released her hand and shifted the champagne glass to shake Michael's. "If not the best man, I'm certainly the luckiest."

Michael placed both hands on Dyana's bared shoulders and kissed her cheeks. "Be happy, Dyana."

Her hands framed his face as she smiled into the dark, sad eyes of the man who had become a major force in her life. "I thank you for helping me to achieve this happiness, Michael," she said. "You've given me things you'll never know of."

"I think I know," he replied.

Jesse Randolph joined the small group, looking elegant in his dark suit. He placed one hand on Nicholas's shoulder and the other on Michael's. "You two men have made this day one of the most important days in my life. My own marriage and the birth of my children come first, of course, but this one comes a close second. And you princess," he said to Dyana, "are the reason."

"If it hadn't been for Dyana," Edna whispered, joining the small group, "Jesse would've never met Michael. It was Michael's money which has allowed Jesse to start over; this time bigger than before, and with the possibility that he may market his sauce nationally."

Dyana did not have to touch Nicholas to feel the tension. Without turning her head, she felt the heat of his gaze drilling her where she stood. Her parents, in a moment of gratitude, had opened Pandora's Box, letting out the suspicions and doubts she and Nicholas had put to rest regarding her relationship with Michael Dalton.

"I think of Dyana as family and there isn't anything I wouldn't do for her," Michael stated with quiet emphasis.

Nicholas's left arm curved around her waist. He wouldn't allow her to escape when his fingers tightened under her breasts.

"It seems as if I've selected quite a remarkable woman as a wife," he boasted. "Quite remarkable indeed."

His words continued to echo in Dyana's brain as she circulated among the guests. Her face began to ache from the incessant smiling, and she slipped out of the living room to a small area which had served as her mother's music room when she lived at home.

She sat in the quietness, massaging her temples with her fingertips. She removed the floral headpiece and laid it gently on the cushion of the love seat. Spreading out the fingers of her left hand, she held them up to catch the light coming through the window. The large stones blazed like the lights in her husband's eyes and she let out a ragged sigh.

The door opened quietly, and it was a moment before she looked up to discover Nicholas watching her. "I was hiding out for a while to get off my feet," she explained when she saw a frown settle between his eyes.

"Don't get up, Dyana," he ordered. "What I have to say should go no further than this room."

Dyana registered the heavy sarcasm in his tone. Her eyebrows rose slightly. "Why the secrecy?"

Pulling over a chair, he straddled it, resting his elbows over the back. "Why did you really marry me?"

The blood rushed to her head, making her weak. Her nerves were taut and instead of crying she laughed. "You're kidding, aren't you?"

Nicholas rested his chin on his hands. "No."

His quiet voice was as lethal as a lashing whip. She would've preferred if he had yelled or screamed because she could've retaliated in kind, letting out her frustration.

"I married you because I love you, Nicholas," she said with all of the emotion she felt for her husband.

"You love me yet you continue your affair with Michael."

His statement caused her rebuttal to lodge in her throat. Her temper flared. "I'm not having an affair with Michael. I never had."

"Why would he loan your parents money? I know what I heard and I know what I've seen, Dyana."

"You hear and see what you want to see and hear," she practically shouted. She concealed her trembling hands in the folds of the gown. "You wine, dine and romance me, believing I had been Michael Dalton's mistress. Why did you chase me, Nicholas? Did you see me as a challenge you couldn't pass up? Did it pump up your ego when I fell for you and you managed to capture the spoils, not Michael?"

Nicholas lowered his forehead to rest on the back of his

hands. The gold band on his left hand stood out in contrast against his brown knuckles.

"Why didn't you come to me for the money, Dyana?"

"Why?" she cried. "So you could believe that I wanted you for your money?" She chewed her lower lip. "I didn't want you to believe I was using you, Nicholas. Don't confuse me with your ex-wife."

She moved, running to the door to escape him. He was faster, capturing her arm before she could reach the hall leading back to the living room.

He caught her bared shoulders and pulled her against the length of his tall, muscular body. Pressing her back to the wall of the narrow passage, he stared down at the tears filling her eyes. His hands curled into fists on the wall over her head while his body held hers prisoner.

"Don't, darling," he crooned when she turned her face to avoid his mouth.

"Don't touch me," she threatened. "With no trust, we have no marriage."

He stepped back from the folds of the swirling fabric of her wedding gown and watched her retreating figure as she returned to the living room, head held high.

The remainder of the afternoon passed in a cloud of whirling confusion for Dyana. Nicholas was the attentive, affectionate bridegroom, none of the wedding guests suspecting a rift in the newly formed union.

They shared a plate as they had the first day at Michael's apartment. Dyana swallowed lamb curry, green beans with water chestnuts and succulent miniature oysters Rockefeller without tasting any of it.

They went through the motions of cutting the cake and exchanging the traditional glasses of champagne. Nicholas drained his glass while she suffered through three sips before handing him hers.

The tossing of the bouquet and garter and it was over.

Susie helped her out of the gown and spread it out over the bed. The suit she was to wear on her return trip to New York hung from a hook on the door of the closet.

"Well, I must say that was the loveliest wedding I've ever attended," Susie stated with a grin. "The bride was lovely, the groom handsome and the father of the bride had tears in his eyes."

Dyana zipped and buttoned her skirt. "He didn't."

"He did. You couldn't see them, but I did." She sat down on a rocker with a yellow and white gingham-patterned cushion. "I'm going to miss you, baby. It won't be the same. How can I cook for one person? And that parrot is more of a nuisance than a pet."

"You still have Michael to cook for on Sundays," she reminded her aunt. "But now that he is retired, maybe he'll come by more often."

Susie began rocking. "I've never counted on a man to keep me company and I don't intend to start now, Dyana Randolph Bradshaw."

Dyana winced when she heard the name. Dyana Bradshaw. She was now his wife.

There was a knock on the door and Nicholas stepped into the room. A light gray suit clung to every line of his tall body.

"The cab is here to take us to the airport."

Dyana picked up her bag and jacket. She smiled down at her aunt, fighting tears. "I'll see you soon, Auntie."

Susie rose to kiss her trembling mouth. "Not too soon I hope. Get used to being married first."

Not even the sight of the magnificent concert piano in the middle of the living room could lessen the pain as Dyana walked into the large manor house. Without asking, she knew the piano was Nicholas's wedding gift to her. The soft, golden light from a floor lamp cast an eerie glow on the black shining surface of the instrument.

She could feel Nicholas's gaze as she stared straight ahead, refusing to reveal any emotion as she yearned to turn and run out of the structure which was to be her home.

The flame that had burned so brightly for her, for them, had diminished and died with his doubts and mistrust.

Raising her chin, she turned her back to walk across the room. "Good night, Nicholas," she flung over her shoulder.

Somehow she made it to the privacy of the bedroom she was to share with her husband before she broke down. She lay across the bed and cried until drained. After a while everything ceased to exist when she fell into a deep, comforting sleep. She didn't stir when gentle hands removed her shoes and outer clothing. A pair of fathomless green eyes examined the dried tears on her face, closing briefly when they swept over the heavy gold ring on the small, delicate hand clutching the pillow beneath the dark brown, red-streaked hair. He pulled a light blanket over her body and turned off the lamp and left the bedroom.

Dyana awoke early, aware of her strange surroundings immediately. The large queen-size four-poster bed was covered with a crocheted-lace bed throw while a shirred fabric in a peach and white print covered the tester instead of the expected canopy. A comfortable reading corner with a love seat and two small-scale pull-up chairs were situated near the window inviting one to relax and read away the hours.

She slipped out of the bed to walk into the sitting room. Peach-colored walls and armchairs and a floral print on the sofa in the sitting room also demanded equal time. The view from this room was breathtaking, and Dyana found herself standing at the window staring down at the flower garden and swimming pool.

Movement caught her attention and she watched Nicholas as he swam the length of the pool with strong, fluid strokes. She was transfixed by the smooth motions he created when his body sliced through the water. Having swam his final lap, he heaved his body out of the water, a muscular chest rising and falling from the strenuous exertion.

She felt like a spy when she hid behind the draperies to watch him. His curling hair was flattened against his head while the water on his skin glistened like shimmering jewels in the bright sunlight. The image of a golden jungle cat, stalking the bush to escape the early morning heat after a trip to the river for a drink, came quickly to mind. He was indeed a magnificent physical male.

He picked up a towel from a table and drew it over his face. He draped it around his neck, but not before glancing up in the direction of the bedroom. She could see his eyes narrowing against the glare of the sun and stepped back to conceal herself.

She retreated from the sitting room to return to the bedroom, her heart racing. It had nothing to do with his seeing her, but from her watching him. Explosive currents sliced through her body and she sank down to the bed. She'd spent her wedding night alone and she wondered if it prefigured the events to come. How long could either one of them exist in a sterile, strained marriage.

She had showered and changed into a yellow sundress when Nicholas found her. She sat on a bluff at the north end of the property, staring out at the smooth surface of the river winding its way northward. The river was crowded with large and small sailing vessels, their brightly colored bows resembling balloons bobbing on the water from the towering height.

Her fingers stroked the satiny fur of the large, friendly cat who lay heavily on her midsection. Buttons had become a mother since she last saw her. The few times she'd come to the house, the feline had remained hidden. The golden eyes opened and closed, always aware of the two tiny kittens as they scampered and meowed with their very tolerant mother. One was black with a touch of white on its front paws and the other was like his mother, a patchwork quilt.

"Come here, baby," she crooned to the miniature black and white kitten. Much to her surprise, the kitten responded alertly to the sound of her voice when it came toward her on wobbly legs. She laughed when the kitten attempted to crawl up her body to be with its mother.

"I think you need some help, little fella."

Dyana almost toppled Buttons to the grass when she

stared up at Nicholas when he dropped the kitten on her chest. He was as silent as a cat.

Shielding her eyes from the sun, she smiled. "Make some noise next time or all of us will become a statistic when we fall off this bluff."

Nicholas sat beside her and rolled over on his stomach. "I'm not going to lose you, Dyana. Not now, not ever."

"But you have," she declared, unable to look directly at him. "You did when you stopped trusting me. What we have is a parody." She sat up, depositing the cat and kitten on the thick carpet of grass. "You say you love me, but that's not enough. You have to trust me. You can't live with the fear that I'm going to be unfaithful to you." She found the courage to look at him. "I know what infidelity is firsthand, Nicholas. It hurts, it wounds. And it leaves scars."

They managed to make it through the first full day together without hostile glares or caustic words. Dyana searched the enormous, ultramodern kitchen and discovered a large walk-in freezer filled with enough food to last them through the winter.

Nicholas prepared the built-in barbecue grill hidden behind a door on the terrace while she marinated steaks for dinner. She showed him how to cut vegetables for a salad and when she observed his dexterity with a knife, suspected he was quite at home in the kitchen.

After dinner, Nicholas took her on a tour of the grounds, pointing out the various trees he had planted since acquiring the property. He showed her the beginnings of a Japanese garden and she smiled when she saw the bonsai plant he had given her when she was convalescing from the auto accident.

All of it seemed normal; except when it was time for them to go to bed. Dyana returned to the bedroom where she had slept the night before and Nicholas disappeared in the direction of the studios.

TEN

They breakfasted together on the terrace in clear weather or in the kitchen when it rained. They discussed magazine business during the commute to Manhattan and on the return trip. They dined out for dinner at least twice that first week, and on the remaining nights Dyana prepared quick, exotic meals. She spent her spare time reading or writing longhand on a steno pad in her sitting room while Nicholas spent solitary hours in his studio poring over the papers he brought home from the office. They appeared the normal couple aside from not sharing a bed.

Nicholas exhibited all of the outward signs of the loving husband in the company of others, setting her nerves on edge whenever he touched her.

He surprised her, and embarrassed Inez one afternoon, when he burst into her office to pull her out of the chair to lift her off her feet.

He kissed her until she was breathless. "Ronnie just called to let me know Carl has been released," he rasped in her ear. "I've made reservations for the both of us to catch a dinner flight tomorrow. We'll leave directly from the office."

She stared at his radiant face. Her arms tightened on his neck and she buried her face against his throat. "I'll be ready."

Dyana secured her seat belt and pulled down the shade to shut out the sun. "I don't like takeoffs," she explained when Nicholas raised his eyebrows in a questioning gesture.

He reached over to hold her hand. "Do you want to change seats?"

"No. It will pass." She swallowed, closing her eyes against

the feel of the aircraft's increasing speed. "How did you meet Carl?" She had to talk; anything to take her mind off the building pressure in the cabin as the plane began its ascent.

"Carl Murphy saved my life in Vietnam," he began softly. "Carl didn't have to go, but he felt it was his duty to serve. Our fathers were both lifers and I met Carl at a dinner given by the top brass in D.C.

"Carl left Ronnie pregnant with their first child when he received his orders. Da Nang, Chu Pong, Khe Sanh, Saigon, Hue or Di An; all the names were the same after a while and so were the horrors. My job was to report the news of the aftermath of battles and photograph the tired faces of thousands of young bronze gods of war who would never be the same from the heat, insects, sniper fire, diseases and the jungle. Their emerald forest became a hell in paradise."

His fingers tightened painfully on hers. "It all became so senseless when more than fifty-eight thousand young, vital Americans died in a nightmare that went beyond description, Dyana. Using my father's connections, I found Carl in a small village and we celebrated our reunion the best we could considering the circumstances. Carl was part of a platoon which was ordered to take a village near Phnom Penh along the Mekong River. We drank black market beer and shared sandwiches filled with something neither of us could identify. Carl was going to throw away his half of the sandwich when a little boy came over to him and stared at it. Carl gave it to him and he bowed and walked away. He couldn't have been any more than eight or nine but he was old enough to handle a grenade. Carl saw what had happened before I did and knocked me to the ground, covering my body with his and taking most of the force from the explosion. Carl lay unconscious, his life's blood soaking the earth while the only blood I shed was from a broken nose when I hit the ground."

"Oh God." She thought of the recurring nightmares Ronnie had told her about. Placing her head on his shoulder, she prayed for him and for the ones who never made it back alive.

He touched her hair with his lips. "Cry for the children, sweetheart. They became the pawns in a sick, useless slaughter. No one trusted them. Most soldiers didn't know whether to smile at them or blow their heads off. They became the innocent, helpless victims, not the men in combat. It bothered me for a long time, but it's over. The nightmares are gone."

Nicholas rushed her out of the airport and she began to feel the tension as much as he did. They entered the waiting area and she recognized the beginnings of a smile lift the corners of his mouth when he waved to a slightly balding man leaning heavily on a cane, favoring his left leg. She stood apart from the two men, watching the emotional meeting. Carl Murphy broke down, his shoulders heaving when Nicholas held him in a tight embrace.

Carl pulled out a handkerchief and blew his nose. His red-rimmed black eyes sparkled when he looked her way. "You must be Dyana."

She returned his smile. "Hello, Carl." She knew all there was to know about this soft, sensitive man.

Carl held her hand and kissed her cheek. "It seems as if all of my Irish luck has been transferred to my good buddy here. I think he lied to me," he whispered. "You're lovelier than he said."

"Thank you Carl. You're very kind."

He waved his hand in the air. "It has nothing to do with kindness. Ronnie told me all about you and I think Nicholas is very fortunate to have found someone like you. Enough chitchat. Ronnie is going to have my head if I don't get you two back before the other guests begin arriving."

Carl did not protest when Nicholas offered to drive his spacious Mercedes sedan to the Murphy home in Alexandria. Dyana sat in the backseat, content to listen to the conversation between the two men and watch the changing landscape as they left the airport for the quiet elegance of the suburban community.

Dusk was descending on the majestic tree-lined street as Nicholas turned off into the driveway of an impressive Tudor structure. Carl escorted her to the entrance of the house while Nicholas unloaded their luggage from the trunk.

Ronnie floated across the floor in an eye-catching black dress in chiffon. The color accentuated the slimness of her body and set off the bright color of her hair which had been put up in an elaborate twist above her long neck.

"Hello again and congratulations," she sighed, holding her arms out to greet them. "I'm sorry to rush you, but the others are due to arrive within the hour. I know that doesn't give you much time to dress, but if you need any help let me know," she sputtered in excitement.

"Calm down, Ronnie," Nicholas suggested. "Come, Dyana, I'll show you our room."

The "our room" did not register until they entered a large bedroom and Nicholas set down the luggage to remove his jacket and shirt.

She stared at the thick dark hair on his chest as he pulled the hem of the shirt from the waistband of his trousers. "What do you think you're doing?"

Nicholas shrugged out of the shirt, placing it on a chair. "What does it look like? I'm undressing so I can shower and shave."

"Can't you dress and shave somewhere else?"

He gave her a long, searching look, then sighed. "Look, Dyana. Just for this weekend we're going to have to put our differences aside. Ronnie has assumed we sleep together because we're married and unless you want to tell her otherwise, you and I are going to have to share that bed."

Differences. His charge that she was having an affair with her ex-boss appeared so insignificant that he looked upon it as a mere difference of opinion.

"Well, if it won't bother you, it won't bother me," she said glibly, matching his mood of indifference.

"You take the bathroom first."

She gathered her clothes from the bag and escaped to the

bathroom, wondering if she would survive the weekend without suffering a nervous breakdown.

Their efforts to dress proved successful when Dyana descended the stairs on Nicholas's arm to enter the brightly lit living room in the Murphy home.

Her heart was slowing from the impact of seeing her husband's penetrating gaze when he emerged from the bathroom to find her dressed in a ruby-red sheath with a provocative front slit allowing for a display of slender legs in three inches of black satin pumps.

His hands were shaking when he attempted to manipulate the bow tie under the collar of the pleated tuxedo shirt, and after the second attempt, she brushed his hands away to tie the length of black in a perfect bow. Her heels put the top of her head at his nose and she kept her gaze lowered to avoid meeting his eyes.

"Thank you for looking so beautiful, Dyana," he drawled softly in her ear.

"The dress helps," she insisted, refusing to look at him.

"It's not the dress, Mrs. Bradshaw," he countered. "It's the woman in the dress."

She gave him a surreptitious glance. Her husband would be certain to receive his share of admiring looks, dressed in a tuxedo with a black tie, suspenders and cummerbund. His longer hair curled over his forehead and she thought that never had she seen him look so appealing.

Waiters and waitresses served the small crowd that had gathered to welcome Carl Murphy home and the tinkling ice in glasses and the occasional laugh indicated the invited were there to celebrate.

Dyana was totally unaware of the picture she presented as she clung possessively to her husband's arm. A pair of large diamond earrings, a wedding gift from Lucy and Dan Chandler, sparkled brightly from her pierced ears, competing with the brightness in her brown eyes. Enough of her slender body was revealed in the clinging red dress to enhance her obvious femininity without appearing vulgar.

All who noticed the handsome couple and hearing that

they had recently married, assumed they were very much in love, with the coy looks they seemed to exchange so often.

Nicholas handed her a glass of champagne from a waiter. "You can pretend to drink it," he said, smiling.

She took a sip, peering at him over the rim of the fluted glass. Was she to spend the rest of her life pretending? Pretend they had a normal marriage? And pretend she could continue as they had the past week? The only thing she was unable to pretend, and that was that she loved him.

"Nick Bradshaw, you sly devil," crooned a seductive female voice.

Nicholas turned and grinned broadly. "Reba Kelly. Where have you been hiding yourself?"

Reba clung to his free arm. "Here, there and about, handsome." Her brown eyes swept over Dyana with deliberate slowness. "I see what kept you rushing out of Washington every chance you got."

"Sheathe your claws, Reba. This is Dyana, my wife."

The brown eyes widened in surprise in a face covered with heavy stage makeup.

"How nice," Reba mumbled.

"Forget her, sweetheart," Nicholas suggested when Reba turned her plastic smile on someone else.

"Done." He pulled her closer and she gave him a open, brilliant smile for the first time since their wedding day. She heard him suck in his breath, then let it out in a ragged shudder. Carl limped over to greet them and the moment was lost.

"Well, friend. You're going to have to advise me on my future as a celebrity. Since my release the phone hasn't stopped ringing. I've received calls from the producers of 'Donahue,' 'Oprah Winfrey,' '60 Minutes' and '20/20,' " Carl informed Nicholas.

Nicholas shifted his eyebrows. "What happened to 'Good Morning America' and 'Today'?"

Carl had to smile. "Allow me to woo the big boys first. What do you think?" he asked.

"Go for it and don't forget to drop hints about your book,"

Nicholas suggested. *"Pinnacle* can use the publicity to jolt a few memories."

Carl nodded. "I can hear the gnashing of teeth at the other publishing houses even now."

"My advice is to take advantage of everything that comes your way, Carl. All the money in the world can't make up for the two years you spent away from your family or their shame and humiliation."

Carl registered his wife's signal. "Dinner is about to be served."

Once seated at the dining room table, Dyana discovered she was not seated with Nicholas, but was flanked by a reporter from the Washington *Post* and the wife of a senatorial aide.

The conversations floating around her were laced with political doings of which she had no interest. Glancing across the table and to her left she saw Nicholas with an expression that indicated he was as bored as she was. His eyes said *I want out,* and she nodded in agreement.

It was only after a seemingly endless parade of different courses and wines that the dinner was concluded. Dyana thanked the reporter when he pulled back her chair. Nicholas circled the table and stood at her side to take her arm.

His hand tightened possessively at her waist. "Ronnie must not have been thinking when she arranged the seating," he whispered.

"Maybe she thought we could stand to be apart for a few hours." She winced once the words were out of her mouth when she saw Nicholas's jaw tighten. How could she forget that they were not normal newlyweds?

"Maybe she's right." His voice held no trace of the gentleness she was used to hearing.

This was the opening Dyana had waited a week for. She wanted to release the anger which had been festering. She wanted to purge herself of the nightmares which haunted her when she lay alone in the large bed each night.

It was either talk about it or leave him.

The thought of leaving Nicholas filled her with a sense of

dread and emptiness. Now it was her turn to wrestle with the images which wouldn't allow her to sleep peacefully throughout a night.

She sat reading until her eyes closed and she woke stiff and cramped. The nights she fell asleep in the bed proved just as restless when she awoke before the sun brightened the sky to signal a new day, staring up at the ceiling in the darkness.

She masked the circles and puffiness under her eyes with an extra layer of makeup, successfully concealing her insomnia from Nicholas, but she knew it could not continue.

Dyana felt as if a weight had been lifted from her heart. She reached a decision: she was going to walk away from the only man she had ever loved.

The assembled sat in the living room waiting for Carl Murphy. He entered slowly, supporting his injured limb with the cane. He stood behind Ronnie, resting an elbow on the back of her chair. He waited until all had been served a cordial, then spoke.

"I wanted to wait until everyone had eaten before deciding to start with the speeches and that is something I wish politicians would learn to do before one's thousand dollar-a-plate dinner congeals before your eyes. I'd like to say a few words to my dear and loyal friends who are gathered in this room to help me celebrate the sweetest freedom a man could ever hope to have. And that is the freedom to be with the ones you love and, above all, trust."

Trust. The word tore at her heart. What good was love if there was no trust?

Carl's dark eyes swept slowly around the room, lingering on each face. "I want to thank you for believing in me and . . . and . . ." He could not continue.

Dyana felt Nicholas's fingers gripping her shoulder. Her hand went up to cover his, wanting and needing to hold him. She did not know if it would be the last time.

She took her time sipping the sweet, thick liqueur, trying to ignore the increasing warmth flooding her face. Nicholas had made no attempt to remove his hand as it moved up slowly to caress the sensitive skin of her nape. Closing her eyes, she reveled in the soothing, hypnotic feel of his fingers as they continued to knead the muscles in her neck.

She had let go of her past, why not he?

"Why don't you go upstairs and get ready for bed," he suggested quietly against her temple. "You look tired."

Tired. She was exhausted. "Are you certain I won't be rude?"

"Of course not."

She stood, offering him her cheek for a chaste kiss. "Please tell Carl and Ronnie I'll see them in the morning."

Nicholas escorted her to the stairs, watching as she made her way to the top and out of sight, and she didn't let out her breath until she was safely behind the bedroom door.

Dyana felt numb from the drugging effects of the differing wines, champagne and from the lack of a restful night's sleep.

She washed her face, brushed her teeth and pulled a demure apple-green, high-neck, short-sleeve nightgown over her weary body. Dimming the bedside lamp, she slipped between the cool sheets and within minutes was asleep.

The side of the bed dipped slightly, causing Dyana to shift toward the other end. She stirred, but promptly settled back into a deep slumber. A soft sigh escaped her parted mouth when a strong arm drew her against an unyielding form. She snuggled against the warm body, seeking its protection.

The heat had become unbearable and Dyana tossed restlessly, struggling to open her eyes. Stretching, she savored the languid sensations in her limbs. She had managed to sleep without the nightmares shocking her into awareness and wakefulness.

She froze, her eyes opening when her brain registered the other body in the bed beside her. The heat was a muscular arm thrown across her back. Shifting slightly, she saw Nicholas asleep on his stomach, one arm over his head and the other holding her virtually captive by its weight.

"Nicholas." His reaction came in the form of a loud snore. She pushed, but could not move him and she could not believe he could weigh that much. But then Nicholas Bradshaw was all muscle and she had read somewhere that muscle weighed more than fat.

Dyana suffered the pressure of his arm until she shifted to where it rested across her hip. She lay motionless until sleep overtook her sleep-craved body a second time. When she awoke again, she was alone in the bed.

Nicholas greeted her with a secret, seductive smile when she refused to look at him.

"You look better this morning than you have in over a week," he remarked, watching closely for a reaction.

"Thank you, darling." The darling came out exactly the way he would say it, the word rolling off her tongue.

Nicholas, amused with her imitation, rose from the chair to kiss her forehead. "You're welcome, darling."

Dyana wanted to tell Nicholas she was leaving him. She had rehearsed the words over and over, but could not bring herself to utter them. It wasn't the time; it never seemed to be the time.

"Nicholas?"

"Yes, Dyana," he replied, not bothering to look up from the newspaper.

"Nicholas . . ."

His head came up and he removed the glasses. A frown creased his forehead. "Is something wrong?"

"I'm going to see my aunt," she said instead.

"Tonight? We've only been back a couple of hours. Aren't you tired?"

She stood, removing the coffee cups from the table. "I'm not tired at all."

"Why don't you wait until tomorrow and we'll go together?"

"I don't want to go tomorrow," she insisted, clenching her teeth tightly. He could not seem to understand that she wanted out, away from him. Now.

"Be reasonable, Dyana. It's almost six and it'll take a couple of hours to drive into Manhattan and . . ."

"Don't lecture me, Nicholas. I know what time it is and how long it takes to get to Manhattan." She slammed the door to the dishwasher. "Don't wait up for me."

Her hands were trembling so much she could not start the car until the third attempt.

Pretend. Pretend all was right; and pretend they would live happily ever after.

Susie took a quick look at her face. "You had your first fight?"

"We don't fight, Susie. We just disagree."

"You're not making sense, Dee."

"My husband thinks I'm having . . . no, had an affair with Michael."

"He what!" Susie appeared as if she was going to faint away. "When did this notion enter his head?"

Dyana was remarkably calm when she related the comments at the wedding reception and her own reaction to Nicholas's accusation.

"And you're saying that you and Nicholas don't . . . don't sleep together?"

"Yes."

Susie took a deep breath of utter astonishment. "The two of you are nuts! Crazy! How long do you think you can go on like that?"

Dyana covered her face with both hands. "Not much longer because I'm getting out."

"And where do you think you're going once you're, as you say, *out?*"

"I'll rent the upstairs apartment from you."

"I don't rent to relatives."

It was Dyana's turn to lose control. "You'd put me out on the street?"

"You have a home, Dyana. And you have a husband who loves you. He may be a little confused as to the facts . . ."

"Facts! Whose side are you on, anyway?"

"No one's side, Dyana Bradshaw. All I want you to do is to go home and talk to Nicholas. Explain everything."

She threw up her hands. "I can't talk to him and I can't talk to you."

The doorbell rang and Dyana's heart began pumping wildly. "If that's Nicholas, I don't want you to let him in."

Susie rolled her eyes. "You forget that I'm the queen of this castle, not you. If I want to let Nicholas in, *I will.*"

Her aunt was a traitor. How could she take his side, knowing what he believed was not true?

Waves of shock slapped at her when she saw Michael with Susie. He had his arms around her as he kissed her flush on the mouth. Something had been going on between her aunt and friend. No wonder Susie did not want her to stay or move back.

"I guess it's out in the open now," Michael stated when he saw the expression on her face. "Tell her, Susan."

Dyana held up her hand. "Don't. Please." She gathered her purse from the table. "I'll see you around."

"Dee!"

"Let her go, Susan. She'll have to work it out by herself."

ELEVEN

She drove around for what seemed to be hours. The needle on the gas gauge wavered on empty and Dyana knew she had to find a service station or check into a motel. She was fifty miles beyond the Tappan Zee Bridge and home.

It was late and everything around her was dark; she had not counted more than a dozen cars going in the opposite direction since she left the parkway.

Nicholas. His name and face crept into her consciousness and she wanted to stop and pick up a telephone to call him. She needed to hear his voice and have him cradle her head to his shoulder. She wanted him to pick her up and swing her around like a rag doll.

He was good for her. He made her smile and giggle like a little girl and he made her want to make love to him like a woman. She was his wife and yet he had not made her his wife.

Her fingers tightened on the wheel when she heard the coughing and sputtering, then nothing. She had run out of gas.

Where was she? Nyack? No, she had passed Nyack hours before and she tried remembering the last sign indicating the number of miles to Albany. It didn't matter because she was going nowhere without gas.

She was too afraid to get out of the car, but she could not sit in it while stalled in the middle of the road. The nocturnal sounds were magnified tenfold, and she tried not thinking of the different forms of wildlife lurking in the nearby wooded areas.

Putting the car in neutral, she managed to push it off the road and onto the shoulder without too much difficulty. But that was short-lived when she realized there wasn't much room in the Corvette for reclining. If she was to spend the night in a car, she would have preferred the spaciousness of the Jeep with its cargo area.

Luck was with her when she found an old sweater in the tiny space behind the seats. Summer was nearing its end with the cooler nights in the northern region of the state. The sweater evoked more memories of Nicholas when she pulled it over her head. The haunting, cloying fragrance of his cologne clung to the fibers and she buried her nose in its thickness and warmth.

She did not bother to roll up the sleeves but pulled them down over her hands like mittens. Flicking the dome light, she noted the time. Two forty-five. She didn't have too much longer to wait for morning. With that thought, she lay down across the seats and tried to fall asleep.

"Is this your car, Mr. Bradshaw?"

Dyana heard the strange voice and opened her eyes to blink against the brightness. She moaned, pulling her cramped legs out from under the steering wheel. From where she lay, she couldn't see the men, but heard their voices.

"It is, Trooper," was her husband's reply.

"It sure is a beaut. Can't blame anyone for trying to steal it."

Steal! Who had stolen his car?

There was a tapping against the window. "All right, Miss, out! And keep your hands in plain sight!"

What was he talking about? She reached over to unlock the door. Her movements were awkward when she pushed open the door to step out.

"I said keep your hands up!"

The uniformed officer was shouting orders at her. Within seconds she found herself spread over the hood of the car, her face pressed against the cold metal.

"What's going on?" she mumbled, tasting dirt and grit on her tongue.

"I think you'd better frisk her, Mr. Bradshaw."

She almost slid to the ground when she felt Nicholas's hands on her body. They roamed leisurely over her back, waist, hips and legs.

"Is she clean?"

He leaned over to peer closely at her face. "Not as clean as she normally would be. But clean enough."

"Okay, you can take her in."

Dyana wanted to cry when she heard them laughing. How could he humiliate her when she had been scared to death. She had spent the night along the road where anything or anyone could have attacked her and her husband thought it was funny enough to stage a mock arrest.

"Let's go home, Dyana."

She tried pulling away from him, but all she succeeded in doing was to wave the too-long sleeves like flags.

"I'm not going anywhere with you," she countered with a return of her spunk. One glance at his face revealed that he hadn't slept or shaved.

His eyes surveyed her critically. "I'm sorry about the joke."

She rose on her toes to thrust her face closer to his. "It's not only the joke, Mr. Bradshaw. It's . . . it's other things, too."

He smiled. "I know. It's me; my jealousy, stupidity and stubbornness. And it's my fault that I've spoiled you, Dyana."

"You did what!"

"Get in the car, Mrs. Bradshaw. It's cool out here and I'm falling asleep on my feet."

"It's out of gas," she drawled.

"Wrong. I put in enough to get us to the nearest service station."

"When?"

"When you were playing Sleeping Beauty, Trooper Griffin drove me to the next exit where I picked up a few gallons."

She looked around for another vehicle. "How did you get here?"

"Ralph Griffin is one of our neighbors. He did me a favor by calling in the description of the car, and when he received word back as to its location he drove me up on his way to work."

She was tired, hungry and too weak to fight him. Even without fighting Nicholas was the victor. "Take me home, please."

The four of them sat silently, staring. Susie looked at Dyana and she looked at Michael; and Nicholas was glaring at Michael.

Michael reached for his hair, but brought the hand down before he could pull it. "I don't want to start shouting in your home, Nick . . ."

"Then don't," Nicholas warned.

"You've got it all wrong. Dyana and I are friends. We've always been friends."

"You don't treat her like a friend," Nicholas countered. "You've kissed and touched her much more than I did before I married her."

"I've known her longer," Michael quipped. He sobered quickly when he saw Nicholas's hands tighten on the arms of the chair. "She's like a daughter. I never thought of her as anything else."

Nicholas still did not look convinced. "You're saying nothing ever happened?"

"No!" Dyana declared. She stared at her husband, daring him not to believe her. "Nothing, Nicholas." She looked over at her aunt. "And I'm ashamed that my aunt and Michael had to become involved in something which we should've been able to work out ourselves. You asked me and I told you the truth. You probably heard things you should not have heard and apparently you believed them. How could I lie to you when I know how it is to be lied to by someone you think you love?"

She left the living room and retreated behind the door of the room which had become a prison and sanctuary. Both she and Nicholas had been surprised when a cab pulled up to the door and Susie and Michael stepped out like avenging angels. Michael began his familiar tirade and Nicholas threatened to call the police to have him removed for trespassing. Susie managed to calm Michael down and Nicholas invited them in.

She had to smile. Michael was ready to wage a war with Nicholas over her honor. He was one of the few remaining knights with a suit of armor which had not tarnished.

Nicholas had admitted his jealousy and stubbornness, but what she had not understood was his reference to having spoiled her.

Dyana heard his footsteps outside of the door, then the knock.

"Come in."

"Is it safe?"

She was forced to smile. "Of course it's safe, Nicholas."

He stared down at her a long time before extending his arms. She did not disappoint him when she rose to meet him. They held each other a long time, healing the rift and washing away the suspicion and pain.

Nicholas picked her up and placed her on the middle of the large bed. Dyana buried her face in his throat, feeling his pulse against her lips.

"I'm sorry," he sighed. It came out like a sob. "Ever since I've known you, it seems as if that's all I know how to say."

"That's not all, Nicholas. You've told me that you love me."

"I'd stopped saying that because I wanted to show you how much I love you, Mrs. Dyana Bradshaw." He pulled her closer and she rested her cheek on his shoulder. "I should've followed the advice I gave you."

"What's that?"

"I told you to forget the past, and I wasn't able to do it. When I heard your mother and father talk about you and Michael, I went crazy. All I could think about was his touching and kissing you. Not once did I think that he saw you as another daughter."

"Michael didn't want me. I never thought he did; but it wasn't until yesterday that I discovered his reason for seeing me. He was after my aunt."

Nicholas sat up. "Susie?"

Dyana nodded slowly. "Yes, Susan Randolph. Now that I think about it, I always thought it was funny that George called Michael's name quite often. I think he overheard things I never got the opportunity to hear."

Nicholas slapped his thigh. "And I thought the bird had an identity problem. He knew exactly what he was saying. Your aunt and Michael must have had some pretty interesting conversations in that kitchen when you weren't there."

"Tell me about it."

He reached out to pull Dyana across his thighs. "Now, tell me what is to happen with the two of us?"

"Well, first of all we are married," she began, counting on her fingers.

"Check."

"And I'd like for us to remain married."

"Check."

She looked up at the arching black eyebrows in a forehead etched with concern. He loved her and she loved him; and it was with this confidence that she remarked, "And I think we should apologize to Susie and Michael for their having to forfeit a Sunday afternoon together."

A deep flush darkened his cheeks under the tan. His wife was not going to be as forgiving as he wanted her to be.

Dyana gave him a look of innocence which melted his anger. "How about if we take them to The Lighthouse?" She smiled when she saw a familiar gleam light his eyes.

"I should've taken your father's advice: put your foot down from the beginning and you won't have to worry about staying married."

Her mouth dropped and eyes narrowed. "Is that what he told you?"

"That was only a portion of what he said which is a certainty to keep a woman in her . . ."

He ducked when she swung a pillow at his head. "Get out!" That is what he meant by spoiling her.

Michael tapped his glass with the edge of a knife. "I'd like to propose a toast, and if Nick doesn't mind I'd like to use one he offered the first day he walked into *Pinnacle* to take my job and my *friend.*" Nicholas acknowledged his claim with a wide grin and nod. "To new beginnings; for all of us."

Dyana took a sip of champagne and smiled across the table at the man she loved. She read the message in his eyes and looked away. Tonight their marriage would begin; with them communicating to the other the depth of their love and commitment.

"Now that sounds very serious, Michael," Nicholas remarked.

Michael's hand covered Susie's. His sad eyes caressed her rounded face. "It is. I've spent almost six years fighting my feelings. I kept telling myself I didn't want to start over with another woman, but I suppose I wasn't too convincing."

Dyana laughed and leaned over to press her lips to Michael's cheek. "When did you decide to throw in the towel and submit?"

"When I went to church with Susan and heard some of the ladies gossiping about some deacon who had his eye on her. I knew then I couldn't waste any more time. Not when I had tasted her cooking and managed to steal a kiss from her every now and then."

Susie pulled her hand away to place it on her hip. "You want to marry me because of my cooking?" Her chest was heaving as her eyes hurled golden bolts of humiliation.

"But . . . but, Susan," Michael stammered. "You haven't allowed me the liberty to sample anything else. I'm certain after we're married there will be other things."

Dyana watched Nicholas as he rested his chin on the heel of one hand, green eyes shifting from Susie to Michael. A knowing grin lifted his mouth in amusement.

"A word of advice, Michael." He ignored his wife's soft gasp. "Marry the woman, and don't acquire the habit of believing gossip. What you'll be forced to forfeit can rival the trials of Job."

"I don't believe it, Nicholas."

"Believe what, darling?"

"That Michael is going to be my uncle."

"Hmmm."

"Nicholas?"

"Yes, darling?"

"You're falling asleep."

One eye opened, then closed. "I didn't get any sleep last night," he slurred. "When Susie called to say you'd stormed out of her place, the nightmares began again. All I thought about was losing you forever." He turned on his side to smile down at her. "You gave me quite a scare, Mrs. Bradshaw."

Dyana snuggled against his chest and pulled the sheet up over their bodies. "Promise me something, Nicholas."

His arm tightened on her waist. "What, love?"

"That you'll never listen to careless whispers again."

"I promise, promise, promise," he whispered against her lips. And he had the rest of their lives to keep that promise.

ABOUT THE AUTHOR

Native New Yorker Rochelle Alers has worked for a literary magazine and taught pre-school, but now enjoys what she loves best—writing romance. *Careless Whispers* is her first romance novel.